A BOSS IN
A MILLION

A BOSS IN
A MILLION

BY

HELEN BROOKS

First published in Great Britain 1999
Large Print edition 1999
Harlequin Mills & Boon Limited,
Eton House, 18-24 Paradise Road,
Richmond, Surrey TW9 1SR

ISBN 0 263 16306 7

Set in Times Roman 16 on 17 pt.
16-0001-59397

Printed and bound in Great Britain
by Antony Rowe Ltd, Chippenham, Wiltshire

CHAPTER ONE

'LONDON? Oh, Cory, don't. Don't leave. Things will work out for you here; I know they will. Just be patient.'

Cory Masters stared back into the face of her friend, her dear friend, the man she had known all her life and loved just as long. How could she tell him that the reasons she had just given for leaving her sleepy little rural home town nestled deep in the green folds of North Yorkshire were lies? The real cause of her intended flight to the anonymity of the metropolis was him, Vivian Batley-Thomas.

Cory smiled brightly, her deep sea-green eyes with their fascinating hint of purple determinedly clear and open and giving no hint of her inward turmoil. 'It's all arranged, Vivian.' She flicked back an errant strand of silky dark brown hair that had blown across her cheek as she continued, her voice cheerful, 'I had the interview a week ago but I didn't think I stood a chance of getting the job when I saw some of the opposition, but then this morning Mr Hunter's secretary phoned. I start in four weeks'

5

time so I can have a few weeks with her showing me the ropes before she leaves to follow her
husband to his new job in the States at the end
of May.'

'But if you were thinking of something like
this why didn't you *say*?' Vivian asked bewil-
deredly, his voice holding a slightly plaintive
note and his boyishly handsome face set in a
dark frown. 'And there's the wedding and everything; Carole was relying on you to help her
with all the arrangements—she just hasn't got a
clue regarding anything practical.' His voice
was indulgent rather than critical and then it
changed as he added, 'You *are* the chief bridesmaid after all.'

'I know.' The smile was being kept in place
by sheer will-power now. If anyone knew, *she*
knew. Chief bridesmaid to the beautiful new-
comer to the market town who had captured
Vivian's heart from the first time he had seen
her at one of the local barn dances. Carole
James, with her long blonde hair and deep blue
eyes, hourglass figure and the sort of legs that
went on for ever. And she was nice too, Cory
thought wretchedly. A bit giggly and helpless,
and she'd definitely never win *Mastermind*, but
nevertheless nice.

'And I can still be Carole's bridesmaid so don't worry. Most of the arrangements can be sorted before I go—that won't be a problem— and you've already booked the church and the village hall with your uncle, haven't you?' Vivian's uncle was the local vicar. 'And I'll be home for the odd weekend before September if there's anything Carole needs help with,' she added soothingly.

'Of course there'll be things she'll need help with.' Vivian's voice was both anxious and irritated, and for a moment Cory's pain was swallowed in anger.

How could he be so...so *thick*? she asked herself silently. They had always lived in each other's pockets from the day they had first started kindergarten together, and with their families living only three doors from each other had spent all their childhood and youth in each other's homes. His parents were almost as close to her as her own. And even when they had gone to their respective universities and met other people none of their relationships had come close to what they had with each other.

Not that anything had ever been *said* exactly. But it hadn't needed to be. She had known he was the one for her and vice versa. Or so she had thought... More fool her, she added bitterly.

'Vivian, I know Carole has no family of her own but your mother will advise in any way she can.' Cory forced her voice to be calm and un-ruffled. 'The village hall is booked for the re-ception already and your mother knows the ca-terers your uncle suggested. There's really no problem. Everything is in hand.'

'But she was relying on your moral sup-port—'

'She'll have you for moral support for good-ness' sake!' It was a snap; Cory's patience only went so far. Her mother was a redhead and in a certain light the deep auburn highlights in her own dark brown hair bore testimony to the fact that she had a good number of her mother's vi-brant fiery genes in her.

'So you really intend to go?' Vivian asked tightly after a small but very pregnant pause, his mouth pulling into a thin line.

'Yes, I really intend to go.' Cory's voice was equally tight. She'd go tomorrow if she could. She'd had quite enough the last few months of watching Vivian billing and cooing with the cur-vaceous blonde, and the engagement party the week before had been an ordeal she wouldn't wish on her own worst enemy. It was over six months to the middle of September, and she would never survive the course if she had to remain in Thirsk all that time. For some strange reason Carole seemed determined to make her her best friend.

'Then there's nothing more to be said,' Vivian said stiffly, and then, in repudiation of that statement, he continued, 'But why you couldn't have put your career on hold for a few more months and carried on working at Stanley & Thornton's I don't know. You say you want a change and that a new job and surroundings will stretch you, and I can understand that at your age—' she'd hit him, she really would, she'd hit him! '—but another six months wouldn't have made any difference in the over-all run of things.'

'Perhaps at my *great* age I didn't think I'd got time to hang about,' Cory bit out sharply as Vivian walked towards the door. Carole, at just twenty years of age, was four years younger than Cory and Vivian and had already pointed the fact out several times in her cute, open-eyed way that made Cory feel like Methuselah. 'Maybe I thought I'd got to grab at life before it passed me by?' Even as she spoke the words she realised there was more than a little self-prophecy in them. She should have left Yorkshire years ago.

Vivian didn't pause in his retreat from her mother's pleasant rose-coloured lounge, and after a second or two, when she heard the front door bang behind him, Cory took a long, deep, reviving breath and forced back the hot tears that were burning the back of her eyes, blinking desperately as she raised her chin high.

No more. *No more crying!* She willed herself to stand perfectly still and for her heartbeat to return to normal. She had cried enough tears in the last few months to fill the ocean and she was tired of feeling so desperate. She was leaving Thirsk in four weeks' time and even if the post of secretary to the illustrious head of Hunter Operations didn't work out—she hadn't mentioned to Vivian or her parents that the offer was conditional—she wouldn't be back to stay. She'd rather crawl through red-hot coals of fire.

All her dreams, all her aspirations since she had first learnt to toddle, had been tied up with the tall, handsome man who had just left the house so abruptly and she was going to have to learn how to face the rest of her life without him, and, having learnt it, to carve a future for herself. It wasn't the path she would have chosen, it certainly wasn't the path that was going to bring her the sort of cosy family joy and harmony she had foreseen for herself, but there had been enough crying over spilt milk and she didn't like the person she was turning into.

Her back straightened and her shoulders pulled back as she emphasised the thought. *She wasn't a whinger.* She'd never been a whinger, and enough was enough. She was young, she was intelligent, and there was life after Vivian Batley-Thomas...gorgeous as he was. No! The last thought had crept in all by itself, and Cory frowned determinedly. She couldn't afford to think like that any more, even for a moment. Gorgeous he might be, available he wasn't. End of story.

'Cory, how nice to see you again, and please, call me Gillian.'

It was a cold April morning four weeks later, and, having taken up residence in her compact but attractive bedsitter the Friday before, Cory had just nervously entered the high-rise offices of Hunter Operations. The building was big, flamboyant and luxurious, and left the neat little offices of Stanley & Thornton's, Engineering Specialists, in the cold, but Gillian Cox's smile was warm and went some way to alleviating the panic Cory was feeling as she faced the chairman's secretary on this, the first morning of the new job.

'Hello, Gillian.' Amazingly her voice sounded nearly normal. 'It's nice to see you again too. How are you?'

'Rushed off my feet, half insane and heading for a nervous breakdown. Other than that, fine.' Gillian's smile widened. She had kindly come to Reception to welcome Cory personally and now walked her over to the lift, saying brightly before pressing the button, 'You must be dying to meet Max; it's not often one doesn't get to meet one's boss until the first day of employment, is it?'

'No.' Cory's voice was weak. She'd thought that herself!

'But he's back from that awful Far East session of conferences and tours, and it's proved very fruitful which is the main thing. And you'll get on fine with him, Cory, really. He's a boss in a million. If it hadn't been for Colin landing such a wonderful job in the States I'd never have dreamt of leaving Hunter Operations, especially after fifteen years with Max, but it's very important to Colin that we begin the cocktail round and so on as soon as possible. You know how these huge conglomerates work,' she added cheerily.

No, she didn't, but she didn't like to say so.

Gillian was still talking when the lift stopped at the exalted top floor and as the doors slid open to reveal lush thick cream carpets and brushed linen walls, the hushed calm was rudely shattered by a very irate, very male voice bellowing, 'Gillian? For crying out loud, woman! Where's that fax from Katchui?'

Cory's eyes shot to the doorway halfway down the wide corridor and to the big dark man filling it, but Max Hunter had eyes for no one but his cool and apparently unruffable secretary who, after a quick aside for Cory to wait in her own office directly opposite them, glided forward, saying calmly, 'It's on your desk, Max, where it's been for the last three days, but no doubt you've buried it under that mountain of paperwork you've been looking at all weekend.'

Gillian disappeared through the doorway but it was a moment or two before Cory could force her legs to take her into the other woman's office, which would soon become hers if this job worked out. Although, having now seen the formidable Max Hunter, she had her doubts about that very thing, she thought a trifle ruefully.

The man in the doorway had been big, very big—at least six feet four—and broad with it. He wasn't old; Gillian had told her Max Hunter's father—who had started the Hunter empire in the late fifties—had died fifteen years ago when his son had inherited at the tender age of twenty-three, but her glimpse of the ˙hard male face and black hair dusted with silver had suggested a man some few years older than his thirty-eight years. And his manner...Cory breathed deeply as she sank into one of the plumply upholstered easy chairs dotted about Gillian's vast quarters. His manner didn't exactly tally with this supposed 'boss in a million' that Gillian had been so enthusiastic about at her interview.

'All's calm again on the western front.' Gillian was beaming as she bustled through the interconnecting door between her office and that of Max Hunter. 'He'd got Mr Katchui hanging on on the phone and Max hates to be anything less than one hundred per cent in control,' she said brightly. 'Typical man.'

Cory nodded without saying anything; she'd gathered that much for herself. She smoothed down the slim pencil skirt of the new navy blue suit that had cost her an arm and a leg, cleared her throat and had just opened her mouth to ask something intelligent when Gillian completely took the wind out of her sails as she leant forward and said, her voice urgent, 'Don't take any notice of how Max is, Cory—his manner and how he talks and everything. He really is a lovely man underneath it all. We've always got on great.'

'You have?' Cory needed every bit of reassurance she could get.

'Definitely.' Gillian nodded firmly. 'But he just takes a bit of getting used to. He's very sure about what he wants and even more so about what he doesn't, and he doesn't suffer fools gladly. Well, he doesn't suffer them at all actually.' She grinned at Cory who bared her teeth in feeble response.

'And he has very rigid views about people,' Gillian went on.

This was getting worse by the minute!

'I interviewed ten applicants on his behalf, you know, and, knowing Max like I do, you were the only one who met his criteria. Some of them were too officious and some not officious enough, one or two had a baby glint in their eyes and dealing with maternity leave and all that paraphernalia would drive Max mad; he's awful to temps. And he doesn't appreciate women who titivate all the time, or clock-watch, and he expects one hundred per cent discretion at all times of course.' She smiled sunnily, her face serene.

'Of course.' Cory gulped audibly. She had to take all this as a compliment that she was the one Gillian had thought fitting, she told herself desperately, but right at the moment it was hard. 'Well, you've told me what he doesn't like, Gillian,' she said carefully. 'Perhaps I'd better know the positive side too?'

And then a deep cold voice brought both their heads turning as it said expressionlessly, 'In essence the five Bs—brains, backbone, breeding, boldness and...' The pause was deliberate.

'And?' She had had to force herself to speak; close to, this man was positively devastating but she dared not let his effect on her show. She had been right in thinking his face was hard, but it was more than that, much more. The dark tanned skin was pulled tight over a chiselled bone structure that was disturbingly masculine, the aquiline nose and strong mouth increasing the impression of severity. But it was the eyes— amazingly beautiful tawny-gold eyes shaded by thick black lashes—which gave his gaze a ruthlessly piercing quality that was totally unnerving and more than a little formidable.

She had never in all her life seen eyes like this man's, and when added to his overall height and breadth—which she now saw was made up of muscle and bone and not fat—and the per-

turbingly cruel nature of his magnetic good
looks the end result was almost paralysing. She
couldn't believe this was her *boss*.

'And beauty,' he finished laconically, and in
the split second before he smiled and moved
forward to shake her hand Cory was conscious
of that golden light shooting right down to her
toes.

She recovered quickly, jumping to her feet
and putting out her hand which was swallowed
whole in his huge fingers, but she made sure her
grip was firm and strong even if her answering
smile quivered a little. She guessed he was jok-
ing about the beauty—Gillian was immaculately
and expensively dressed, and her greying hair
was expertly cut in the latest style, but not even
her nearest and dearest could have called the
homely-faced woman remotely beautiful.

'So you're the paragon Gillian was so de-
lighted to unearth,' he said thoughtfully. His
voice had a smoky, husky tone and a faint ac-
cent she couldn't quite place, and was utterly in
keeping with the dynamic whole. It made her
toes want to curl.

'I'm Cory Masters, Mr Hunter.' She had re-
trieved her hand as soon as possible; the feel of
his hard, warm flesh was not improving the state
of her nerves. 'It's very nice to meet you.'

'Likewise, and the name's Max by the way,' he returned easily.

Max. How on *earth* was she going to be so familiar as to call him by his first name? Cory thought feverishly. The thought was daunting.

'Short for Maximilian,' he continued imperturbably, only a slight narrowing of the brilliant gaze suggesting he was aware of the hasty withdrawal. 'My father liked to tell the tale that I was christened after one of his favourite film characters, Maximilian the robot, in the film *The Black Hole*?' Cory had never heard of it but she nodded anyway. 'But he admitted privately the name came from the Roman emperor Maximilian I, and that it is from the Latin maximum meaning greatest.' He eyed her lazily, his mouth quirking.

Robot or Roman emperor, the name fitted, Cory told herself with a faint touch of hysteria. He was easily the most overwhelming individual she had ever come across, and she had committed herself to work for this man as his secretary-cum-personal assistant. She must be mad! She was way, way out of her league here.

'Now, I understand from Gillian that for the next couple of weeks you are mainly going to observe and digest,' he said coolly. 'The following month you will assist and hopefully by the last week will have become autonomous. Ask any questions you like, dig, delve, call Gillian in the middle of the night if you feel so inclined, but don't bother me. I don't know how the office out here works and I don't want to; that's what I pay a secretary for. I expect you to be able to put your finger on anything I want at a moment's notice, and I never accept excuses. Is that clear?' he added smoothly.

'Perfectly.' There was something in his tone that had put Cory's back up although she couldn't have explained what, and now she found herself saying, before she could stop herself, 'I take it from this morning's incident that you expect your secretary to be as fully conversant with every item on your desk as she is of her own?' She had kept her tone pleasant, even conversational, and in the pause before he spoke again she could almost see the razor-sharp brain trying to assess exactly where she was coming from.

'Absolutely,' he agreed with apparent unconcern, but again the amber eyes had narrowed just the merest iota and Cory knew her little jibe about the buried fax had been received, analysed, and filed away under the correct heading of sarcasm.

Which made her crazy, she told herself in the next instant, when after a curt nod of his head he turned and disappeared back through the interconnecting door, shutting it sharply behind him. Why start off on the wrong foot right from word go? Oh, she should have kept her mouth well and truly shut! She was her own worst enemy. Her father was always saying the same about her fiery, volatile mother, and somehow in Max Hunter's authoritative presence all her father's calm, placid genes had died and all her mother's reckless ones had come rushing to the fore.

'Right.' Gillian's voice was neutral. 'Let's get you acquainted with all the companies under the Hunter Operations umbrella first. There's a breakdown on that desk over there with all relevant facts and figures. Most of it is confidential. I've also done a rough précis of the main people, both within Hunter Operations and without, whom you're likely to deal with, and any background—hang-ups, problems, difficult to communicate with or easy, that sort of thing—to help you along a bit. Could you destroy those sheets in the shredder once they're in your head because at least half of them would feel inclined to have me up for libel if they read them?'

'Thank you.' The other woman's smile was infectious and it made Cory feel a little better, although she found her hands were trembling when she took the seat at the desk Gillian indicated. Max Hunter was probably congratulating himself right now for the trial period stipulated in the job offer, she thought grimly, smoothing back a shining strand of dark hair which had escaped the prim French pleat at the back of her head, and she couldn't really blame him. But she intended to make sure that if, or perhaps she should say when, he decided not to make her a permanent offer he wouldn't be able to use the quality of her work or her dedication as the excuse.

Cory was deep in a very interesting and, she had to admit, somewhat aspersive review of Max Hunter's current main competitor when she heard the buzzer on Gillian's phone. 'Yes, Max?' There was a moment or two of silence and then, 'Oh, yes, that's fine with me. I'll just check... Cory?'

Cory lifted her head enquiringly to Gillian's slightly bemused voice, and saw the older woman was staring at her with a studiously blank face which gave absolutely nothing away.

'Max was wondering if you are doing anything for lunch? He suggests taking us to

Montgomery's as a little celebration of your first day at Hunter Operations. I'm free, are you?'

'Montgomery's?' The name meant nothing to Cory—she had only been in London just over a week—but from the other woman's tone it clearly wasn't a fast-food restaurant. 'Yes, that would be lovely,' she managed faintly. And then, once Gillian had relayed their acceptance, she asked, 'What exactly is Montgomery's, Gillian?'

'It's a restaurant,' Gillian said carefully. 'A very…nice restaurant. I've been there once or twice before and the food is very good.' She was trying to be offhand but the message was clear.

'Right.' Cory's heart sank still further. No doubt men like Max Hunter took their secretarys to such places all the time, but she hadn't had Gillian's experience. She just hoped she didn't let anyone down. This was probably some kind of a test?

The remainder of the morning sped by as her brain tried to assimilate a hundred and one facts, and just before twelve, at Gillian's urging, she made use of the little pink and white cloakroom attached to the secretary's office to freshen up before lunch.

'What are you doing here, Cory?' She took a long breath as she stared at the wide-eyed girl in the mirror. The discreetly elegant hairdo, the circumspect make-up, the expensive suit and Italian leather shoes—this wasn't her. Who was she trying to fool? She wasn't going to carry this off, no way, no how. She should never have tried for this job—it was way, way out of her league. Huge, anxious, sea-washed green eyes looked back at her, and she gave a nervous swallow in the same moment she realised the palms of her hands were damp. Calm down, girl. Calm down.

She had to carry this off. She continued to stare into the mirror as she gnawed at her bottom lip, and then hastily splashed cold water over her wrists before re-touching her make-up and spraying a few drops of perfume on to cool skin. She had her bedsit now, and in spite of the fact that it was only one large room tucked away in an old house in Chiswick it was costing a small fortune. She needed every penny of her six-week probationary salary, but Gillian had stipulated a hundred per cent increase once the position became permanent, and that would be good money—very good money. Of course she could get cheaper accommodation, but she had fallen in love with the lovingly restored

Victorian house with its gracious sense of the past, and her bedsit—right at the top of the house and affording a panoramic view over roaming rooftops and a huge expanse of light-washed sky—was an oasis of peace amidst London's bustle.

'Cory?' Gillian's voice just outside told her it was time to go, and she took a hard, anxious pull of air, smoothing down the fitted jacket of the linen suit and tweaking the collar of her jade-green blouse into place before she left the small sanctuary.

The two women had just slipped on their coats when the door to Max's office opened. He moved lazily towards them, his powerful body possessed of an animal grace that was entirely natural and all the more formidable because of it. There was no polite 'All ready?' or any other preliminary small talk; he merely gestured with one hand towards the outer door, his hard-boned face cool and closed, and as he did so Gillian's telephone began to ring.

'Leave it.' It was an order and Gillian nodded, but then, after her answering machine had cut in and just as Max was closing the door behind him, they heard a man's voice say after the beep, 'Gill? Gill, if you're there pick up the phone, love. It's urgent.'

'It's Colin.' Max had already swung the door wide again and as Gillian hurried to the phone with a muttered, 'I'm sorry,' he leant lazily against the outer wall in the corridor outside, his gaze switching to Cory with alarming suddenness and pinning her to the spot. She stared back at him, willing her nerves not to show.

'How was the first morning?' he asked in that husky dark voice that sent her nerve-endings into hyperdrive.

'Good.' She nodded in what she hoped was a brisk fashion, and prayed he would put her burning cheeks down to the central heating which was of the hothouse variety. This was stupid, this was so *stupid,* Cory told herself angrily as she frantically searched her blank mind for something to say. She was supposed to be working for the man from nine to five—or six or seven, whatever the day demanded—five days a week, but at this rate she wouldn't survive the day, let alone the first week.

She had been so composed and cool and calm at that initial interview back in February. The pain and misery of Vivian's engagement party two days before had been so vivid in her mind that a kind of numb fatalism had guided her through the ordeal of Gillian's hundred and one questions and practical tests; she'd felt then that the worst that could possibly happen had happened, so what was the success or failure of a job interview compared to Vivian marrying someone else? In fact she'd still felt like that right up until... When? *This morning at nine o'clock.* When she'd looked into a pair of narrowed tawny eyes set in the coldest face she had ever seen. And also the most attractive, she added wryly.

'Good?' He drawled the word slowly with a hint of mockery. 'Care to elaborate on that enigmatic statement?'

No, she wouldn't, and she wasn't mad about his supercilious attitude either. Funnily enough the thought brought two of Max's aforementioned Bs—backbone and boldness—into play, and she heard herself saying, her voice firm now and aiming at polite reserve rather than the cutting coldness she would have loved to display, 'It would be foolish of me to venture an opinion after just three hours, don't you think? But certainly Gillian has been extremely helpful and kind.' She raised her chin and straightened her shoulders.

'It would be impossible for Gillian to be anything else.' There was genuine warmth in his voice for the first time and it made the smoky effect lethal. 'She's a secretary in a million.'

'That's just what she said about—' Cory stopped abruptly. She wasn't at all sure Gillian would appreciate her repeating her earlier comment, besides which, this man's ego was big enough as it was. But it was too late. He'd homed in like a nuclear missile.

'About?' he questioned softly, but she knew they were both aware of what she had been about to say. It was there in the eyes.

'About you,' Cory admitted grudgingly. 'She said you were a boss in a million.'

'And you doubt that very much.' The hint of laughter was unmistakable. Cory was too surprised to do anything but stare at him, her green eyes with their mercurial violet tinge wide and her full-lipped mouth slightly agape as she searched her mind for a response.

Max Hunter seemed to be enjoying himself. She watched him settle more comfortably against the wall, and there was a definite measure of satisfaction in the deep voice when he said, 'True or false?' as black eyebrows rose mockingly.

He was as unlike her previous employer as it was possible to be! The thought flashed through Cory's head and brought small, strutting Mr Stanley, with his formal, ritualistic working mode and almost phobic fear of any relaxing of office protocol or decorum, there in front of her for a moment. He would no more have a conversation like this with his secretary than fly to the moon! Mind you, she wasn't Max Hunter's secretary, not yet, and perhaps he never intended for her to be? Perhaps she didn't *want* to be? And she agreed with Gillian's statement—Max Hunter was certainly a boss in a million all right. It was just the way he'd earned the title she and his secretary differed on, Cory thought caustically.

It was the last thought that opened Cory's mouth and enabled her to say, with suspect sweetness, 'I'm sure Gillian is absolutely right, Mr Hunter, when she says you're one on your own?'

'Max,' he corrected smoothly, 'and I've been insulted less prettily in my time. Do you work as well as you fence, Cory?'

She wasn't going to win a war of words with this man. For the second time in as many minutes Cory found herself with her mouth open and she shut it quickly with a little snap. 'Better,' she said brightly. This job was a nonstarter. She knew it.

'Then we'll get on just fine.' He levered himself straight.

It was as he turned to face the doorway through which Gillian was walking that Cory noticed the scar on the right side of his neck. It was long and jagged, starting above his ear in his hair and disappearing down into the collar of his shirt, and spoke of a savage accident. The scar itself was silver but due to his dark tan it stood out quite distinctly from the surrounding skin, and for a moment or two Cory couldn't take her eyes off it. She had averted her gaze by the time he turned to her again, but it had really shocked her. What on earth had happened to him?

'I'm sorry I've kept you both waiting.' Gillian was flushed and flustered, and when her voice wobbled a little and she added, 'It's Colin—he's not well,' Max took the older woman's arm as the three of them entered the waiting lift.

'What is it?' he asked with surprising gentleness. 'What's wrong?'

'Oh, nothing, not really.' Gillian breathed in deeply. 'A touch of food poisoning, they think. Colin says it's not serious.'

'But you're missing him, and no doubt he's missing you.'

'Uh-huh.' Gillian nodded and then managed a fairly normal smile as she included Cory in her rueful grimace. 'Pathetic, isn't it? But the last eight weeks are the first time we've been apart in our twenty years of married life and it feels so strange. Still, at least Colin's found a gorgeous apartment out there and everything is going to be done when I arrive on the doorstep in six weeks' time.'

Six weeks. *Six weeks!* And then—if she was still here, that was—there would be only Max Hunter and herself and no comforting, homely Gillian around. Cory missed her step as she followed the older woman into the lift and immediately a warm firm hand fastened on her elbow. 'Careful.' He was just behind her and his six feet four towered over her five feet five as she turned to murmur her thanks. 'We don't want you breaking your neck on the first day, do we?' he added evenly. 'And certainly not in this building. I can do without a lawsuit for industrial injury.'

'I wouldn't *dream* of suing you for something that was my own fault,' Cory answered hotly as though the accusation were a reality.

'No?' It was blatantly cynical, his firm, cruel mouth twisting mockingly at the fierceness of her protest.

'No.' She stared up at him, her mouth very firm, and they were both unaware of the interested spectator watching the little drama in front of her. 'That would be positively immoral.'

'Immoral...' He considered the word lazily.

Cory was instantly aware she had chosen an unfortunate turn of phrase but it was too late to retract it. She'd have to bluff.

'And you are always...moral, Cory?' he asked quietly, with hateful butter-wouldn't-melt-in-my-mouth innocence.

'Always.' This wasn't going to work. This job *definitely* wasn't going to work. For some reason he didn't like her; there was veiled antagonism in his every word, his every glance, and she wasn't imagining it. He had been gentle, understanding even, with Gillian, but with her it was almost as though he was trying to catch her out all the time, Cory thought tightly. He was a cold, hard, macho *brute* of a man—everything she detested in a male, when she thought about it—and she hadn't made the move to London to live in a perpetual state of tension and stress.

'Then Gillian has chosen well.' It wasn't what Cory was expecting and she was eternally glad the lift chose that precise moment to open its silent doors and deliver them in Reception. 'Now, a nice relaxing lunch, I think?'

His voice was even and distant suddenly, and, ridiculous though it was, Cory felt as though the man now escorting Gillian and herself through the ingratiating smiles and nods in Reception was an entirely different creature from the one she had seen so far. He was cool and remote and self-assured, every inch the powerful tycoon and entrepreneur, as he strode through the hushed and immaculate surroundings and out through the gleaming brass and glass doors which one of the reception staff had fallen over themselves to open.

A blue and silver Rolls-Royce was parked at the kerb outside the building with magnificent disregard for yellow lines, and as Max led the two women towards it Cory had the notion she was taking part in a flamboyant movie, and any moment a director would be leaping in front of them and shouting, 'Cut! It's a take.'

The chauffeur had opened the rear door of the limousine the moment he had caught sight of Max, and now, as Cory followed Gillian into the rich leather interior, she wished there were a little more room in her skirt. Discreet, calf-length and prim it was, cut for scrambling in and out of breathtaking vehicles like this one it wasn't, and she was vitally conscious of Max Hunter just inches behind her and no doubt with his eyes on the material straining over her backside.

She was hot and pink by the time she was seated next to Gillian, but then, as Max joined them on her other side and his hard male thigh rested against hers, she knew what a pressure cooker felt like. He was her boss. He was just her boss. Say after me…

If her life had depended on it Cory couldn't have told anyone how long it took to reach Montgomery's, the route the Rolls took through the heavy lunchtime traffic or even what the three of them discussed *en route*. Every fibre of her being, every cell in her body was concentrated on not making the biggest fool of herself ever, but she must have sounded fairly coherent and behaved normally because Gillian's nice round face was quite cheerful and relaxed when the limousine eventually glided to a halt outside the sort of establishment that just reeked of class and wealth.

Of course the glass of champagne might have helped. When Max had leant forward and opened the polished wood cocktail cabinet in front of their seat Cory had determinedly stopped her mouth from falling open—twice in one morning was quite enough—but her eyes had widened all the same. The glasses were tall

and exotic and chilled, the champagne was pink
and frothy and tasted like all the summers she
had ever experienced rolled into one, and Max's
toast—'A welcome to the newest member of
Hunter Operations'—brought the colour that
had just receded from her cheeks flooding back
again.

'I don't remember you doing this for me
when we first started working together, Max?'
Gillian had already said, with her first sip of
champagne, that it would go straight to her
head, and certainly as her employer helped both
women out of the car Gillian was as flushed as
Cory as she grinned at Max.

He smiled easily. 'I wasn't sure how to treat
a secretary in those days, Gillian, if you remember. I've learned as I've gone along.'

Cory envied the other woman's quiet famil-
iarity with their boss. Of course Gillian was a
good few years older than Max and very happily
married to boot, and she'd known him for years,
but Cory just knew she would never, *never*, be
able to adopt the almost motherly approach that
Gillian did so well and which, at heart, was the
basis for all good boss/secretary relationships.
He just scared her to death. He did what?

Immediately the thought formed she caught it
in horror. She wasn't frightened of Max

Hunter—she'd never been overawed by any man, even her old headmaster who was a tyrant of the first order and had scared everyone rigid. She was *not* frightened of Max Hunter! That was the most ludicrous, stupid, crazy notion she'd ever had! It was the champagne. It had to be the champagne.

'Cory? Is anything wrong?'

Gillian's gentle voice brought her out of the whirling maelstrom of her thoughts, and to the realisation that she was standing in the middle of the crowded pavement with people weaving around her. Hardly the pose for a young, dynamic secretary!

'Shall we?' Gillian gestured towards the building in front of them and as Cory's eyes focused on Max she saw he was holding open the door of the restaurant, an expression of great patience on his face, but it was the look in the beautiful and compelling amber eyes that bothered her. They were narrowed and intent and piercingly steady, and they brought to mind a wildlife programme she had seen just the other night, when a quite magnificent tawny-eyed lion had been watching his prey—a delicate and fine-boned wildebeest—with frightening and fierce single-mindedness.

And then he blinked and smiled, heavy lids and thick black lashes sweeping down, and when he looked at her again he was just an unusually arresting and powerful man. A man any woman would think worthy of a second glance, a man of intimidating intelligence and undeniable presence but, nevertheless, just a man.

The meal was simply wonderful, and seated as they were in a quiet and private alcove, where they could see and yet not be seen, Cory found herself relaxing enough to enjoy the good food. From the moment they had been seated Max had set out to be a charming and amusing dinner companion, keeping the two women entertained with a monologue of witty and slightly wicked stories, and by the time Cory had spooned the last delicious morsels of feather-light crêpe Suzette into her mouth she had been lulled into a comfortable state of false security.

So it made it all the more shocking when, Gillian having disappeared to the ladies' cloakroom a moment or two earlier, Max turned to Cory and held her eyes with his own as he said calmly, 'Well, Cory? Have you decided whether to turn tail and run or stay yet?' He raised those cruel black eyebrows again.

'*What?*' It was too loud—she knew her voice had been too loud and that was quite the wrong tack to take with this man. She needed to be calm, unflustered and in control, she thought feverishly as she watched him settle back in his seat and continue to survey her through slits of brilliant light that brought the poor wildebeest to mind again. Although at least on the plains there was somewhere to run.

He was the sort of man who was intimidating even when he wasn't intending to be, and she wasn't sure if he was intending to be now or not. He was so *big*, that was part of the problem—so masculine and uncompromisingly virile. Everything he did, every little gesture or movement, was so controlled and disciplined and it was formidable. He had an aura of authority, but not in a comforting or reassuring way—at least she didn't find it so, Cory told herself nervously. Hunter by name and Hunter by nature...

Oh, for goodness' sake, girl, pull yourself together! The rebuke was loud and angry in her head. She'd be crediting him with supernatural powers next and wouldn't he just love that?

The thought acted in much the same way as a douse of cold water on her fluttering panic, and Cory forced herself to take several silent breaths before she smiled and said, her voice as

cool as she could make it, 'I really don't know
what you are talking about, Max.'

There, she'd said his name without the
slightest pause or hesitation, even giving it a
slightly scornful intonation.

'No?' The gold was very clear around the
bottomless black pupils. 'You mean to say you
weren't considering whether you'd come back
tomorrow or just call it quits?' he asked silkily.

'No, I wasn't.' And she hadn't been, not really. Admittedly she had wondered whether *he*
would pull the plug on *her*, but she hadn't se-
riously considered leaving herself. Whatever
else, she wasn't a quitter, and she said so now.
'I agreed to take the position for a trial period
to see if things worked out and I would honour
that whatever,' she said firmly. 'And it works
both ways—*you* might decide I'm not suitable,'
she added reasonably.

'I knew within the first five minutes whether
you were suitable or not,' he said softly. 'In
business you have to be able to determine the
credibility of someone fast.'

'Snap decisions?' She raised disapproving
eyebrows and hoped he hadn't guessed she was
acting a part—his previous admission had sent
her stomach haywire and churned up that wonderful lunch.

'No, measured appraisals due to years of hard experience and a natural distrust of my fellow man,' he corrected her swiftly, his tone faintly mocking. 'I never make mistakes, Cory. Not any more.'

'Oh, you used to be just like the rest of us, then? Human?' The second the words were out she was horrified. You didn't speak to your employer like that, she told herself silently—not if you still wanted him to remain your employer, that was. Mr Stanley would have had a heart attack on the spot! But Max Hunter wasn't Mr Stanley.

'You see?' There was a measure of amusement in the narrowed eyes and she knew her embarrassment was showing. 'I'd rather have you in my corner than someone else's. Besides which...' He paused, swallowing the last of his coffee in one gulp before he continued, 'As my secretary and personal assistant you'll be working with me very closely and of necessity the days are often long ones—eleven, twelve hours. I couldn't stand anyone who didn't speak her mind and I don't like boring women, Cory.

'I can forgive anyone anything if they are honest and acting from the heart. I don't like deception or hypocrisy and I don't like prissy thinking along the lines of ''the boss is always right." I *am*—' he eyes were gleaming with laughter now '—but if you thought so too, where would the spark be? And you don't have to like me, so don't worry your head on that score,' he added abruptly. 'Because you don't, do you?'

It wasn't a question, it was more of a statement, and one which Cory was utterly unable to answer.

He laughed out loud now at the look on her face and the sound was husky, rusty even, as though he didn't do it too often.

'Don't get concerned,' he said softly, his voice soothing. 'Believe it or not I look on that as another of your admirable attributes. Part of Gillian's amazing success all these years has been because she has her Colin whom she adores to distraction, and our working relationship has been just that…a working one.'

He was telling her he didn't want her fancying him! Cory didn't know whether to be relieved or furious, but she veered towards the latter. What an ego! What an outsize, monstrous ego!

'Power and wealth can be a potent aphrodisiac to some women. Now, whilst that's all to the good in certain situations—' the deep voice held a note that suddenly made her shiver as her nerve-endings sensitised '—at work it's just a damn nuisance and sometimes downright dangerous. You'll be party to some very confidential papers as my secretary and the old adage of "Hell hath no fury" is still alive and well, believe me,' he finished coolly.

'Mr Hunter.' She had probably been as mad as this previously in her life but she couldn't remember it. 'I would no more dream of acting in the way you've described than of…of flying to the moon,' Cory snarled angrily. 'Even if I thought you were the best thing since sliced bread.'

'Which you don't,' he put in softly, his eyes gleaming.

'No, I don't!' she affirmed with furious emphasis.

'You see? The perfect solution for both of us. I get a secretary I can trust and who—from the references Mr Stanley among others supplied— is more than adequate not to mess anything up with misplaced emotion. You get a position which will only serve to further enhance your career, you get to travel a bit, see new places with the added advantage of it all being paid for, and a handsome salary to boot. Ideal, eh? And of course you're out of the little home-town trap. Why exactly did you decide to leave

Yorkshire anyway?' he added with a suddenness that took Cory by surprise. 'You were happy there for the last twenty-four years.'

She stared at him a moment, getting a bland, expressionless gaze in return, and then forced herself to speak quietly and calmly when she said, 'It was time to spread my wings, that's all. My qualifications are excellent—' she raised her chin slightly at this point; it didn't come naturally to blow her own trumpet '—and at twenty-four I felt the next stage of my career was overdue. I—'

'I'm not asking for a résumé of what was written on your application form and CV.' He was terse. 'I mean the real reason. Was it a man?' he asked with audacious coolness.

Cory was quite unaware of the shadow of pain that passed over her face in the second before the fury hit, but then her eyes were shooting bright green sparks and she straightened in her chair, her chin thrusting out and her hands clenched fists in her lap. 'I think I ought to make one thing perfectly clear before we go on another minute,' she said icily, her voice belying the fiery colour in her cheeks. 'I do not discuss my personal life with anyone unless I want to. If you offer me this job permanently you will be entitled to all of my working days and the very best I can do, both for you and Hunter Operations, but you will not automatically have the right to take over my life. My private life is my own business and absolutely no concern of yours.'

So it *had* been a man. Max Hunter surveyed the taut, angry figure in front of him, his face betraying none of his thoughts. And she wasn't over him yet, not by a long chalk. 'You're absolutely right of course.' Gillian was making her way back to their table and now he stood, his voice merely pleasant and not at all put out as he added, 'I think we're all ready to leave? And Cory?'

She was in the act of rising, Max having pulled out her chair for her, and now, as she turned to face him, he was so close for a moment that she caught the scent of delicious aftershave on clean male skin and took an involuntary step backwards, bumping against the table and rattling the coffee cups. 'Yes?' she asked defensively.

'The offer *is* permanent; it was from five past nine this morning.'

CHAPTER TWO

THE next few weeks were something of a revelation to Cory, not least because she found, after the initial couple of days which passed in a tangled blur, that she was actually enjoying her job. No, enjoy was too weak a word. She was *loving* it; she couldn't wait to get to the office every morning, and that in spite of the million and one facts that were thrown at her every minute—or so it seemed—the hours flew by on winged feet.

She had had her good days and bad days at Stanley & Thornton's, and her position as secretary to the managing director had been both an interesting and extremely responsible one, but working for Max Hunter was something else. And that was the understatement of the year.

Nevertheless, on the morning of Monday, the seventeenth of May, when Cory awoke to clear blue skies and brilliant sunshine, and the realisation that from this day on it was just her juggling the hundred and one balls that Gillian had seemed to manage so effortlessly, she felt more than a little nervous and the butterflies in her stomach were going crazy.

Not that Max Hunter had been anything other than completely professional and detached from that first lunchtime, she reminded herself quickly as she flung back the covers and knelt on her bed to look out of the big picture window at half of Chiswick's rooftops. And patient when he'd had to be, calm, unruffled—at least with her. However, she suspected he'd made a special effort during her settling-in period, and with Gillian there—who practically seemed to read his mind and know what he wanted before he knew himself—he'd had no reason to be anything else. She had observed enough to know he was not a naturally patient man, also that his bark could be every bit as bad as his bite with lesser mortals who stepped out of line.

'Do...not...panic.' She spaced the words out slowly, her heart hammering. 'You're going to be fine, just fine.'

Of course, if she was being *absolutely* honest, it didn't help that he often worked at his desk with his jacket off and his tie loose or flung aside altogether. She nipped at her lower lip, shaking her head at her own absurd foolishness. It shouldn't matter, she *knew* it shouldn't matter—he was only her employer for goodness' sake—but the first time she had walked into his office, on her second day at Hunter Operations if she remembered rightly, and seen him frowning over a load of scattered papers on his huge desk, his massive shoulders and broad physique accentuated by the thin blue silk shirt he was wearing, she'd done a double take.

Thank goodness he had been more interested in the report he'd been looking at than her entrance, she thought now, as her cheeks flushed at the memory of how she had felt.

His tie had been hanging either side of his collar on that occasion and the first two or three buttons of his shirt had been undone, revealing a hard tanned throat and just the beginning of a smidgen of body hair below his collar bone, and she hadn't been able to believe what it had done to her.

Not that she was attracted to him. The thought was fierce and one which came into play several times a day without fail. Not in the slightest. It was just that after little Mr Stanley, with his bald head and paunch and unfortunate tendency to sniff all the time due to chronic catarrh, Max Hunter's particular brand of aggressive male virility was something of a shock. But she'd master what was after all nothing more than an animal response, a fleshly, purely physical thing. Of course she would. No problem.

She just hoped it would be sooner rather than later, she admitted to herself the next moment with a deep sigh. This stupid...awareness of him made her jittery and nervous, and although she was careful to hide it she was constantly on edge in his presence.

Cory breathed in and out a few times, her gaze wandering round the big light sun-washed room, and coming to rest on a huge cake tin perched on top of the small fridge in the minute kitchen in one corner of the bedsit.

She had been home for the first time this weekend, and before she had set off back to London, her mother had packed her faithful little Mini with enough food to keep an army for a month.

Her brow wrinkled as she thought of the two days she had just spent in Yorkshire. She had relished the time with her parents—she had always been close to the pair of them and they had had a riotous evening out on the Saturday when all three of them had eaten and drunk far too much—but meeting Vivian again for the first time in six weeks had been hard. Well, more than hard if she were honest.

As soon as he had spied her bright red Mini parked outside the house on Saturday morning—she had travelled down late on Friday night after Gillian's farewell party—he had been knocking at the door, and it had been all of three hours before she could get rid of him. *Get rid of him?* The thought stopped Cory in her tracks as she made to walk across the room. She'd never want to get rid of Vivian, would she? She hadn't meant it like that, not really. It was just that she felt awkward now he was engaged to Carole—that was it—uncomfortable and unsure of how she should behave. And he had seemed so...unhappy? *No.* The denial was immediate. Of course he wasn't unhappy, just harassed with all the wedding arrangements and so on. And that was perfectly understandable; of course it was.

She shook her head slightly as she walked across the room. She was going to have a shower in the small bathroom across the landing directly opposite her door, and then fix herself toast and coffee before she got ready for work. She had plenty of time—she had woken a good hour before her alarm was due to ring—but she wanted to get into the office nice and early and have Max's post opened and ready for him on his arrival at Hunter Operations. She intended to start as she meant to carry on, and that would involve one hundred per cent commitment. But that was all right—certainly for the next few years at least. The last thing, the *very* last thing she was looking for after the heartache of the previous few months was a romantic involvement of any kind. Work was safe—you knew where you stood with career ambitions and the like—it was men who were the unknown quantity and liable to cause you heartache and grief.

A pair of hard amber eyes suddenly shot into the screen of her mind and she paused, her hand outstretched towards the big bath sheet on the little stool by the door, as she told herself that was different. Max Hunter was her boss, that was all, and any nervousness or flutters she felt about him were quite legitimate when you considered her financial security was in his hands. And that was the only reason, *the only reason*, that this magnetism problem was getting to her. It was. For definite.

Cory arrived at Hunter Operations at a quarter past eight, but when she walked into her office and looked through the open interconnecting door into Max's domain she realised he must have been in residence for half the weekend, from the amount of papers strewn about his desk and floor. The man was a workaholic!

'Good morning.' His voice was preoccupied. And she had opened her mouth to make the necessary response when he continued, 'Can you be ready to fly out to Japan this evening?' His tone suggested he was asking for nothing more unusual than a cup of coffee.

'Japan?' The therapy of a leisurely soak in hot bubbles followed by toast and coffee on her tiny balcony immediately vanished as she gazed at him in amazement.

'Uh-huh.' He didn't raise his head as he spoke but she saw he was frowning at the papers in front of him. 'This deal with Katchui is getting too complicated; I need to get over there and sort a few things out face to face. You can't beat flesh contact.'

He looked at her then, two piercingly sharp rays of golden light holding her to the spot before he lowered his head again. 'Two first-class tickets any time after three this afternoon; see to it, would you? And I need some coffee, black and strong, and a sandwich. Ham, turkey, beef—not salad or cheese. I need nourishment, not punishment,' he added dryly.

'Right.' She tried to make her voice brisk and secretarial rather than bemused and stunned, which was how she felt.

'And I need that tape on your desk typed up before midday; if we need to make any changes we'll have to do it before we leave.'

'How…how long do you expect us to be away?' Cory asked faintly. Talk about life in the fast lane; this was express mode.

'Five days, a week at the most.' Again the amber light raked her face. 'It's not a problem?' It was said in a tone that suggested it had better not be.

'No, no, of course not.' A week in a foreign country with Max Hunter for company? she thought weakly. And he asked if it was a problem? But it went with the territory and she had known that when she'd accepted the position; it was just that she had expected a few more weeks to get…acclimatised.

The morning sped by on winged feet, and once she had presented the report for Max's eagle-eyed scrutiny at just gone eleven Cory dashed back home and frantically threw clothes and other necessities into a case, dug out her passport, and was back in the office before twelve and straight back at work.

It was almost half past one when it suddenly dawned on Cory that she hadn't let her mother know about the trip, and she had just dialled the number and heard the receiver being lifted at the other end when Max chose that moment to put in an appearance with a sheaf of papers in his hand and a preoccupied expression on his face.

Blast! Cory heard her mother speak the number and didn't like to put the phone down. He *never* came to her; in all the weeks she had been at Hunter Operations the buzzer had invariably summoned Gillian into the inner sanctum. She spoke quickly into the phone. 'Hi, it's Cory. I'm just ringing to let you know I'm going on a business trip to Japan for a few days, so don't worry if you ring the house and there's no answer.'

'Japan?' Her mother was all agog. 'How exciting, dear. I'm glad it wasn't this weekend anyway; we had a lovely time, didn't we? It was wonderful to see you; your father and I so enjoyed it.'

'It was wonderful to see you too,' Cory said uncomfortably, vitally aware of the big dark figure on the perimeter of her vision.

'And Japan, you say? Well, well. Now make sure you take some travel sickness pills—you know how you are—and—'

'I'm sorry, I'm going to have to go.' She knew, without looking at him, that he was scowling. There were dark vibrations coming across the airwaves. 'And I'll look after myself, don't worry. I'll phone you as soon as I get back.'

'All right, darling, and thank you for letting us know. I hope everything goes well and that you have a lovely time. Love you.'

'Love you.' It had been their stock goodbye all through her days at university and since she had been in London and Cory didn't think twice about it. Until she raised her head and looked into Max's face, that was.

'Quite finished?' It was expressionless and even but she knew exactly how he meant it, and immediately she rebelled. He had told her in the first week that the making and receiving of private calls was quite acceptable, as long as she chose the appropriate time and didn't talk to her long-lost cousin in Australia every day, but this was the first call—the very first call—she had made. And she wouldn't have had to do that if he had given her more notice about the Japan trip, either! Well, he certainly needn't think he was browbeating her or making her feel guilty, she told herself hotly. Even Mr Stanley had allowed her more licence than this.

'Yes, thank you.' It was cold and curt and told him his attitude had been noticed and was not appreciated.

'Then perhaps you'd do a better job on these predicted sales figures than Mr Mason's secretary has. I can only just work out what they mean and I don't expect Mr Katchui to have to wade through columns and columns of unnecessary rubbish.' His voice was clipped and terse, as though she were the one at fault. 'Whatever we're paying the woman it's too much,' he finished on a growl.

'Right.' Cory's jaw was set as she took the proffered report. 'We will need to leave here no later than half past two; the flight is at four.' Her voice was as terse as his and just as cold.

She had been so busy concentrating on avoiding touching his hand that her grasp on the papers was minimal, and as the last page became adrift and began to fall she made a grab for it at the same time as Max bent to retrieve it. They didn't exactly make contact, but as her brow brushed against his and the warmth and smell of him encompassed her the effect on Cory was like a powerful electric shock, and the rest of the papers fanned out in a graceful arc about his bent head as she shot backwards.

'Oh, I'm sorry.' This time her lunge forward resulted in their heads cracking together with enough force to make Max see stars for a moment or two, and she was aware of her illustrious boss staggering a little and saying something extremely rude before he took a visible hold of himself and said, 'Leave them, leave them for crying out loud. I'll do it.'

Cory took a very long deep breath as she watched him bend his knees and gather up the pages, and she tried to ignore the way powerful shoulder muscles bunched under thin silk and the way the pose brought expensively cut trousers tight across lean thighs.

'Thank you.' It was succinct in the extreme but all she trusted her voice to say. She was just grateful it wasn't a croak.

'My pleasure.' He glared at her once on straightening before banging the crumpled papers on her desk and turning on his heel, disappearing through his door and slamming it behind him.

Wonderful, absolutely wonderful. Cory stared after him as she willed her heartbeat to return to normal. Not content with aiming to knock him out once, she'd had to go back for a second shot at the title! She bet she knew what he was thinking as he sat in there: Come back, Gillian;

all is forgiven. The thought brought a weak smile in spite of her embarrassment. In all the six weeks she had been with Gillian she had never once seen the older woman anything but composed, placid and patient when dealing with her volatile boss. Well, they said variety was the spice of life…

Max didn't risk poking his head out of his office until ten minutes before they were due to leave and, as luck would have it, just as she typed the last number on the neat and concise sales figures she had displayed clearly enough for a child to understand.

'Just finished,' Cory said brightly as she pressed the print key. She didn't look directly at him; she just couldn't.

He walked across to her desk and stood waiting a moment without speaking, and then, as she handed him the first methodical and compact page of figures, glanced at it intently before raising his eyes and giving her one of his rare and devastating smiles. 'Excellent. You've checked it all?' he asked briefly.

'Yes.' She didn't add that she'd found several of the columns on the original report had been wrong and that she'd had to go back to Mr Mason to confirm what was what. She had an idea that his secretary wasn't going to last long anyway.

'Right.' He had put down the first sheet of paper and was fastening the collar of his shirt and pulling his tie into place as he said, 'Time to get moving, I'm afraid. You're all ready?'

Ordinary though his actions had been, there was a curious intimacy to them that Cory couldn't have explained but which made her cheeks flush, and now she busied herself tidying the other printed pages and handing them to him as she said, 'Yes, I'm ready.'

Was the rest of his body the same golden-brown as his face and throat and arms? With his great height and muscled lean frame he must look pretty sensational unclothed... A sudden shiver at the thought awoke her to what she was thinking, and she was weak-kneed with relief that he had turned and gone back to his own office to fetch his things, shutting the door behind him.

What was the matter with her? she asked herself faintly. Had she gone stark staring mad? She couldn't afford to harbour any thoughts like that about Max Hunter. It was all the more disconcerting because she had never, ever let her imagination run riot with anyone else, even Vivian. But Vivian wasn't like Max. The

thought opened her eyes wide as she plopped
down on her seat and then leapt up again to tidy
her desk and fetch her suitcase and jacket from
her washroom, all the time telling herself she
was his secretary, his *secretary*, for goodness'
sake, and she would be out on her ear if he so
much as caught a glimmer of what she was
thinking. He would misconstrue it, think she
fancied him or something, and she didn't. She
didn't. She *really* didn't.

Due to a last-minute call from the States and
then one from Mr Katchui himself, Max didn't
join her in the outer office until nearly three, but
the drive from the offices in Brentford to
Heathrow was straightforward and Max's chauffeur drove the car competently and fast through
the heavy afternoon traffic.

The couple of package holidays Cory had
been on in the past just didn't prepare her for
the sort of treatment afforded the exalted first-
class passengers, but she couldn't enjoy it to the
full with every nerve-ending screaming. It was
being *with* him like this. He was obviously the
type of man who automatically took care of the
woman he was with, and although it was nice—
it really was—to be folded into him by his arm
round her waist as he used his body as a barri-
cade to protect her in the chaos of the terminal,

not to have to carry her heavy case, to be whisked through the usual mind-numbing red tape in a way that made her breathless, it was disconcerting as well. In fact it was more than disconcerting if she was truthful.

And she was vitally aware of the little stir his presence caused among the female contingent too—not that Max seemed to notice. The older women and the very young ones weren't too bad—the former discreet and the latter somewhat awestruck, but there were a couple of predatory females in the VIP lounge in particular who were quite blatant in their appreciation. And it rankled. The more so because they totally ignored her as though she didn't exist.

Once on the plane—and never in her wildest dreams had she imagined air travel could be so luxurious—Max's jacket and tie were immediately discarded and he settled back in his seat with all the appearance of being utterly relaxed. 'Take your shoes off, loosen anything that needs loosening and prepare for a long journey,' he drawled lazily as the amber gaze took in her tenseness. 'We're nearly twelve hours in the air and the time difference means we land around midday Tokyo time. We're meeting Mr Katchui late afternoon, and it's going to be a long twenty-four hours whatever way you look at it.

Once we've eaten try and catch a few hours' sleep.'

Cory nodded carefully. Yes, she'd try, and she would also aim to be the efficient, cool secretary a man in his position had the right to expect, she told herself flatly.

Sexual chemistry had its places, but the office was not one of them, she reflected soberly as she undid the buttons of her thin linen jacket and eased her court shoes off her feet. She just didn't recognise this side of herself when she thought about it. She had never considered herself to be a particularly sensual person; her love for Vivian had care and fondness and warm affection at its core, and of course she had thought he was a very attractive man, she added quickly. Very attractive. But there had been no stirring of her senses, a little voice in her head reminded her, or at least not in the same way as Max Hunter got under her skin.

'And don't look so worried.' He leant across as he spoke, his voice low and soft as Cory sat rooted in her seat. 'I would never have taken you on as my secretary if I didn't think you were up to the job. You may not have noticed but I'm not a natural philanthropist.' And then, when she just stared at him, 'That was meant to be amusing but don't feel obliged to smile just because I pay your salary,' he added with dry self-mockery.

'Don't worry, I won't.' It had been his nearness that had frozen her reaction—he had been so close she could see the little black regrowth of his beard beginning to show through the tanned smoothness of his chin and smell his aftershave, which was a subtle blend of something wicked, but now she forced a grin as she spoke and was rewarded by an answering quirk of his mouth.

'No, I didn't think you would.' He'd settled back in his seat and now the amber eyes narrowed, and he surveyed her for a good ten seconds before he added, 'Whoever he is, he isn't worth all the heartache, Cory. Take it from someone who knows.'

'What?' Her mouth straightened as her eyes widened in surprise. 'Who on earth are you on about?' she asked ungrammatically.

'This bozo who's been giving you the runaround.' His voice was quite without expression. 'Because he has, hasn't he?'

'I really don't have the faintest idea what you're talking—'

'What's happened?' he continued evenly, ignoring her interruption with his normal arrogance. 'Has he suddenly realised his mistake since you've been down in London and talked you round?'

'No one has talked me round,' she said indignantly.

'It doesn't look like that to me.'

What on earth was he talking about? she asked herself silently. He didn't know anything about Vivian, did he? Not that there was anything *to* know, she added bitterly. There never had been, not really. It had been a one-sided love affair in every sense of the word. 'Max, I'm telling you, no one has talked me round,' she insisted jerkily. As far as Vivian was concerned there had never been anything to talk *about*; she was just good old Cory, friend, comforter, confidante, mug. *Mug?* Where had that come from?

She didn't have time to explore the shock declaration her mind had thrown up before Max said, his tone astringent, 'Then why did you tell him not to worry about you and that you love him?'

'I told Vivian I *love* him?' The words were out before she had got her brain engaged, but he seized on them like a dog with a bone, his eyes glittering and his mouth tight.

'Vivian? Is that his name?' It was magnificently scornful but he didn't seem as pleased that he was right as normal. 'I've always thought it far more appropriate for a woman than a man,' he said scathingly, 'but then I suppose it depends on the type of man.'

This was getting out of hand. Cory took a deep breath and prayed for composure. 'Max,' she managed to say quite calmly, 'I think we're getting our wires crossed here.' The phone call. The flipping phone call! 'I haven't talked to Vivian since the weekend and I certainly haven't told him I love him. If you're referring to earlier in the office I was talking to my mother.'

'Your mother?' He blinked once and she had the rare—the extremely rare—opportunity of seeing Max Hunter lost for words.

'Yes, my mother,' she answered, her tone tart, but inwardly the sight of her esteemed and authoritative boss literally gaping was really rather satisfying. 'You didn't give me much notice about this trip if you remember,' she continued coolly, 'and surprisingly I do have a life outside Hunter Operations, and there are people who might worry about me if I don't answer my phone for a week.'

He recovered almost immediately. 'Like the aforementioned Vivian?' he asked pointedly. 'The name did slip off your tongue.'

Why, oh, why had she been so foolish? She stared at him in exasperation as she wondered how much to tell him. He was watching her closely, observing her reaction in that big-cat, unnerving way of his, the pale amber shirt he was wearing accentuating the vivid gold of his eyes and increasing the impression of an animal about to spring. Oh, get a hold of yourself, woman! She forced herself to lean back easily in her seat as the thought hit. Max Hunter was a man who liked to hold all the cards—she had seen enough of the way he operated over the last six weeks to know *that*—and as far as he was concerned his secretary was an appendage of himself and therefore as much under his control as his own right arm.

Gillian's life had been an open book—marriage at twenty-five to her childhood sweetheart, and a mutual decision, on finding out that they couldn't have children, to put all their energies into their careers—and that was fine...for Gillian. But she didn't see that a baring of her soul had any relevance to the way she conducted herself as Max Hunter's secretary.

'Vivian is a friend,' she said at last, her voice flat. 'A dear and old friend and I have known him for years. Okay?'

'No, it isn't.' And then, as her eyes turned a dark jade and the violet tint was eclipsed by stormy grey, he added, 'I need to know you're with me, one hundred per cent with me, Cory, and that's the bottom line. I don't need a secretary who's pining from unrequited love or anything of that nature; it just won't do. It would affect your work and you know it.'

'How dare you?' She glared at him angrily. This was too much.

'I dare because it is necessary,' he said grimly, and never had the dark, brooding quality to his powerful charisma been more evident. 'I rely on my secretary too much to be mealy-mouthed.'

'Look, Max...' She paused, biting back the hot retort she had been about to make as several thoughts flashed through her mind. He was paying her a very good salary—an excellent salary—and the experience and credibility she would gain as his secretary and personal assistant would be enormous. There were hundreds of girls out there—probably just as well qualified as her—who would bite Max's hand off if he offered them the chance of working with him. All in all he probably had every right to demand that one hundred per cent commitment, and it wasn't a problem anyway. It really wasn't a problem! So why hadn't she bitten the bullet and told him so?

'Vivian is a childhood sweetheart who is marrying someone else,' she said flatly, 'and I am not—*I am not*—pining for him.' And she wasn't. The knowledge hit her like a ton of bricks and made her voice shaky as she continued, 'I want to make a success of this job, I really do, and you are going to have to take that as read because I am not going to beg and plead to try and make you believe me.' She looked at him straight in the eyes as she spoke.

'You don't have to.' Suddenly his voice was amazingly soft. 'Can I ask you one more thing?'

She nodded. She would have liked to have said no but her courage wasn't endless and the sooner this was finished the better.

'If he asked you for another chance tomorrow and meant it, what would you say?' he asked gently. 'And the truth, now.'

'I don't know.' His face was intensely sexy. It wasn't the moment to have such a thought but it was there and Cory just went with the flow. It was so strong, hard-boned, and the dusting of silver in his jet-black hair brought an experience to the magnetism that was lethal. How many lovers had he had in his time?

'You don't know?' He shook his head slowly, his mouth quirking. 'How long do you think you have loved this guy, Cory?' he asked quietly. 'This soon-to-be-wed childhood sweetheart?'

'Forever.' It probably wasn't tactful but it was the truth.

'Forever?' He echoed her words with another shake of his head. 'And yet if he came grovelling tomorrow, declaring undying love, you'd have to pause before you knew whether you would be prepared to take him on or not?' he asked pointedly. 'Is that right?'

Put like that it sounded awful. Cory stared at him, her green eyes mirroring her confusion as her creamy skin flushed with hot colour. Why did he have to twist things like that?

'Cory?' he prompted determinedly. 'Is that right?'

'You're twisting things.' It was weak but it was all she could manage through the whirling bemusement his probing had caused.

'Am I?' He smiled slowly, his eyes warm.

And then everything in her life before was reduced to nothing, and all her concepts of commitment, love, prudence, discretion were blown to smithereens as he leant forward and his mouth descended on hers, his gaze never leaving her face. His lips merely brushed hers in a light, momentary touch that was over before it had begun, and then he had reclined back in his own seat again and shut his eyes before she could say anything or even move, his voice very even as he said, 'The guy is an idiot who doesn't deserve you and you know it at heart. Forget him and get on with your life, Cory. You're young and beautiful and it's time to move up a gear and have fun. Work hard and play hard for the next few years; there are plenty of fish in London's pool and you don't want to splash around in the shallows forever.'

He had kissed her. Cory was eternally thankful that the shudders of sensation that continued to flow from that one brief embrace were hidden, but even so her face was scarlet and she was glad Max's eyes were shut. And yet you could hardly call that fleeting, transitory contact a kiss, she told herself in the next instant as the voice of common sense took over. Take hold, Cory.

He had meant it as an encouraging conclusion to their conversation, as his final words had proved, a positive statement for her future, and it had meant as little to him as a pat on the back. It wasn't his fault that she had found it... devastating. But she had. Oh, she had. She just couldn't help it.

She leant back in her own seat and shut her eyes, willing her burning cheeks to return to normal. No, it *was* his fault, she told herself crossly some seconds later; he was just so totally *male*. There were some men whom women would find it easy to regard as friends or colleagues and have platonic relationships with, there were others who, due to their attractiveness or sexual charisma or whatever, made the comrade thing a little harder to achieve, and then there was Max Hunter. He was one on his own, there was no doubt about it, and it wasn't just she who thought so either, she comforted herself silently. She had seen his effect on the female of the species over the last few weeks and it was blistering. He reduced the most intimidating, hard-boiled businesswomen to purring pussycats when he *wasn't* trying, and when he was... Well, he was lethal. And he knew it and used it too.

She nipped at her bottom lip, finding it a relief to admit to herself at last that she was just like every other female and fancied him rotten. But he was her boss and therefore the main work colleague she would be dealing with day after day, and this attraction she felt—which was a purely physical thing and as such could be controlled with a little will-power—had to be kept strictly under lock and key. He had made it plain, ruthlessly plain, on her first day at Hunter Operations that all he wanted in a secretary was an efficient, pleasant and intelligent machine—any gooey feelings or romantic inclinations would mean she would be out on her ear faster than she could say Jack Robinson.

She nodded at the thought, feeling a surge of adrenalin that she now saw things so clearly. She had it all under control, of course she did, and that was good—very good. There was no need to panic or get alarmed. She could be as cool as the next girl.

The kiss having been put in its proper perspective and the little pep talk finished, her mind turned back to the disturbing revelation she had had about Vivian. Did she really think he had taken her for a mug? she asked herself with determined honesty. The answer was loud and clear. She hadn't been imagining all those times he had waxed lyrical about the future, their future, even if he hadn't been specific. And the kisses they had shared, his tenderness, his reliance on her. She had cosseted him and fussed over him, and when she had been at university and had had the odd date or boyfriend—something they had both agreed they would do—it had been as if he'd been there with her, as a silent and condemning spectre. He'd always gone quiet and hurt when she had spoken of other men, in spite of the fact he had been seeing girls himself, and she had *fallen* for it, she admitted now with silent wrath. She had, completely.

And he had still continued to manipulate her after he had shown an interest in Carole. He had behaved as though she was his protected baby sister from that point, turning things around and weaving his little threads of half truths until she had been convinced she had misunderstood their relationship in the past. How could she have been so *stupid*? She had to stop herself from grinding her teeth. She would have respected him much more, admired him even though she might have felt hurt, if he had come right out at the beginning and admitted he had fallen in love with someone else and out of love with her. She could have handled that.

She should have seen all this; she couldn't understand why she hadn't. Why had it taken a comparative stranger, Max Hunter, to point out the obvious? What was the matter with her?

'What a fierce little face.' It was cool and mocking.

Her eyes shot open and she turned her head to see the amber gaze casting its golden light over her face. 'I...I was just daydreaming.' She defended herself quickly. 'That's all.'

'I'm not going to ask what about,' he said with dry amusement. 'I've a feeling I'd rather not know. The stewardess has just left the menu for dinner; perhaps you'd care to take a look?'

Menu. They had a proper menu in first class? Oh, how the other half lived! Cory took the proffered menu with a smile of thanks and determinedly cast her eyes downwards.

Okay, so the more she *seemed* to know about men, the less she actually knew, but what the hell? This luxurious plane journey was a first and she was going to enjoy it with all her might. She wasn't at all sure about how her feelings stood with regard to Vivian, but one thing she did know—she had done the right thing in leaving Yorkshire and spreading her wings. Whether it had been right to fly into Max Hunter's particular net was another matter entirely, but only time would tell if she had jumped out of the frying pan into the fire.

She cast a sidelong glance at Max from under her eyelashes and her stomach gave a little lurch at his closeness. There ought to be a law against one man having so much going for him, she thought winsomely, her mouth turning up at the edges. But at least she was safe from any weakness and temptation where he was concerned. He wanted a secretary. End of story. And she ought to be thanking her lucky stars that was so, because she wasn't at all sure she could have trusted herself should he have decided to turn on the charm. And Max was the eternal bachelor. She'd bet he'd broken hearts all round the globe.

'There is what could safely be called an enigmatic smile about those rather beautifully shaped lips.' Her eyes shot to his face and as far as she could tell he hadn't opened his eyes. The big body was quite relaxed, his limbs outstretched and his breathing steady and controlled. 'Would it do me any good to ask what you were thinking about?' he drawled lazily.

'No.'

'I thought not.' He shifted slightly and she felt the movement in every nerve and sinew. 'Choose your meals and then settle back and relax,' he suggested evenly. 'You're too tense.'

Oh, how right he was!

CHAPTER THREE

THEIR plane touched down at Narita, Tokyo's international airport, just before midday, and they were through the green route system with the minimum of fuss to find Mr Katchui's car and chauffeur waiting to whisk them to their hotel to freshen up before they went on for the initial meeting at the Katchui building.

Cory had only indulged in the odd catnap on the journey—she had been too excited and nervous to relax into a deep sleep as Max had done—but nevertheless, in spite of the tiredness that was beginning to make itself felt, she was eager for her first glimpse of Tokyo once the narrow agricultural belt around Narita had vanished.

The city was huge; five million people travelled back and forth to work each day and it was not unusual for the tidal wave of humanity to spend four hours a day in travelling, Max informed her as he watched her drink in the vast urban sprawl.

'Four hours?' Cory stared at him aghast. 'The poor things.'

'In any other country there would be bedlam, but here patience and self-control are instilled in children from birth, and everyone treats everyone else with great respect.' Max sounded as though he approved, and this was borne out when he continued—leaning against her slightly as he gazed out of the window, which caused her some difficulty with her breathing, 'The city divides into self-contained little villages and towns, each with its own remarkable flavour and ambience, and the excellent subway system puts them all within minutes of each other. Everything is run with superb efficiency.'

'A city after your own heart?' Cory couldn't resist asking.

'When it embodies virtually no street crime and petty theft like this one, yes.' He had caught the faint trace of sarcasm in her voice and his voice was slightly curt as he relaxed back into his share of the seat, but he continued to fill her in on the background of the areas they were passing through.

It was as they passed the Shibuya district that their driver spoke in rapid Japanese, his head slightly bent their way, and Max answered him just as rapidly before turning to her and saying, 'He wants me to tell you the true story connected with the Shibuya station; everyone in

Tokyo knows it. Hachiko, an Akita dog, used to walk with its master who was a university professor to the station each morning and meet him each night, but then one day he didn't return. He had been taken ill and died. The dog waited for the last train and then sadly returned home, only to repeat the journey every evening for seven years until it too died. The people of Tokyo were so impressed by the little dog's faithfulness that they paid for a bronze statue to be placed just outside the station.'

'Oh...' Cory stared at Max as a vision of the loyal little animal filled her mind. 'That's so sad.'

'In a way.' He was looking just beyond her out of the car window and although it might have been a trick of the light she thought his eyes were shadowed when he added, 'It's certainly an indictment on human beings' concept of fidelity.'

'Oh, I think most people are capable of faithfulness given the chance,' Cory returned lightly without really thinking much about what she was saying as she turned back to the scene beyond the car.

'Do you?' Now something in the tone of his voice brought her head swinging back to face him, and although his face was quite expressionless and his eyes clear the grimness was still there when he said quietly, 'I would have to disagree. Monogamy is one of the most spurious myths we higher animals perpetuate, and the enforcing of it causes more misery than all the wars in the world put together. People strive for the impossible and then blame each other when they can't achieve it.'

It was clear he meant every word and Cory was so taken aback for a moment that she simply stared at him, her large green eyes tinged with dismay before she managed to say, 'That's a hard way of looking at loyalty and devotion, isn't it?'

'Realistic,' he answered briefly, his eyes taking on a cold metallic stoniness. 'Where a man and a woman are concerned anyway.'

She knew she ought to leave it—they had been travelling for what seemed like for ever, and the May day was warm and humid and far from over—but it was beyond her. 'I don't think so,' she argued quietly. 'I know lots of couples who are perfectly content to be faithful and never look at anyone else.'

He shook his dark head slowly, his eyes never leaving her hot face. 'Now that has to be one of the most presumptuous statements I've heard for a long time; how on earth do *you* know whether they are content or not? And you certainly wouldn't know if one of them was indulging their more carnal appetites away from home, now and then. Most people do aim to be at least a little discreet,' he finished fairly irritably.

'So according to you the whole world is nipping in and out of bed with every Tom, Dick and Harry, or at least yearning to?' Cory asked heatedly, resenting the implication that she was naive.

He surveyed her without speaking for a moment, a touch of amusement in his face at her indignancy, which made her want to hit him, and then said, his tone lazy now and holding a smile, 'I don't know if "nipping" is quite the word, and certainly I've never been tempted to indulge with a Tom, Dick or a Harry, but the basic principle is there, yes. Of course it is.'

'What utter rubbish,' Cory said pithily as his patronising attitude hit her on the raw.

'Rubbish?' He couldn't have reacted more strongly if she had reached out and slapped his face.

Well, at least he wasn't amused any more, Cory thought a little uneasily as she saw the patronising expression replaced by sheer rage. She doubted whether too many people had ever told Max Hunter to his face that he was talking rubbish. But she stuck to her guns. 'Yes, rubbish,' she repeated a trifle nervously. He really was annoyed and the space in the car had suddenly seemed to shrink by a few feet. 'I admit that city life is different to the rural scene and you are probably basing your opinion on your own set of acquaintances and friends, but certainly in my home town I know loads of people who have been married for twenty, thirty years, and are as happy as Larry,' she finished defiantly.

'Leaving aside this Larry—' his tone was acidic in the extreme '—are you honestly telling me that you can be absolutely sure that these paragons of virtue are living in a state of wedded bliss?' He eyed her grimly but she refused to be intimidated.

'Yes,' she shot back sharply. 'I can.'

'Cloud-cuckoo land.' It was said with apparent resignation and sorrow that she could be so naive, and Cory found she didn't trust herself to speak. Telling your employer he was speaking rubbish was one thing; informing him that he was a condescending, supercilious, male-chauvinist pig was quite another. She turned back to the vista of grey ferroconcrete offices, factories, warehouses and huge housing developments outside the window and prayed for calm. She couldn't lose her temper; it would accomplish nothing.

And then she thought of something and turned to Max, her voice as flat as she could make it, and said, 'Do you know if this faithful little dog was a male or a female?'

Golden eyes held aggressive green, and she read the answer before a sardonic voice said, 'When the story was first told to me the animal was referred to as female.'

Cory nodded thoughtfully, her voice quite expressionless as she said, 'Yes, I'm not surprised.'

It was a tentative victory, but in the circumstances Cory was willing to take whatever she could get.

Their stylish hotel in Ebisu was part of a new leisure development on the former Sapporo Brewery site, and the richly decorated public areas and guests rooms were both luxurious and impeccably clean.

After all the hours of travelling Cory couldn't resist a quick bath in the exotic, beautifully tiled bathroom, and as she slipped on the cotton yukata provided for guests' use, prior to getting dressed, she glanced at herself in the mirror.

She didn't look tired, she reassured herself, before stepping forward and scrutinising the flushed, bright-eyed girl in the mirror. She had released her hair from its refining clip and now it rested on her shoulders in a thick, silky, gleaming mass, her creamy skin and sea-green eyes throwing her vivid colouring into warm prominence. Max had never seen her with her hair loose...

The thought came from nowhere and it shocked her into jerking away and moving into the bedroom where she dressed with record speed, before scraping back every strand of hair into an eye-wateringly tight knot at the back of her head which she secured firmly.

Max was in the next room, and when he knocked at her door some fifteen minutes later she had been ready and waiting for most of them. She was doubly glad she had had the time to compose herself fully on her first glimpse of him standing nonchalantly in the doorway. He had obviously taken the time to have a shower; his thick black hair was raked back from his forehead in its normal severe style but it was still damp, a small tendril or two curling forward and giving the hard masculine face an elusive touch of boyishness that was dynamite.

'All ready?' His brief smile was preoccupied.

'Yes, I'll...I'll just get my bag,' she said quickly.

Cory was hoping and praying she was up to the demands of this trip. The luxurious flight, the effortless efficiency with which they had been whisked to their hotel, the palatial surroundings had all further impressed upon her that she was up among the big boys where perfection was paid for and expected, and she was suddenly terrified was she going to let Max— and herself—down. Gillian had been so experienced and professional, she was never, ever going to rise to his previous secretary's standard, she thought with a sickening lurch to her stomach as she reached for her bag and thin linen jacket. And out here, in a foreign country, she felt so vulnerable.

'What's the matter?' Max's voice was quiet and direct.

When she turned to face him again he had stepped into the room from the corridor beyond and was looking at her intently.

'The...the matter?' It was soft and trembly and not at all the way an executive secretary-cum-personal assistant should talk, and Cory forced her voice into a firmer mode as she added, 'I don't understand. Nothing is the matter. I'm fine, just fine.'

'Liar.' For such a big man he moved very lightly, even fluidly, and the two or three strides to reach her side were made before she could blink. He lifted her chin with a determined finger, regarding her steadily for some moments before he said coolly, 'Are you nervous about the forthcoming meetings and all they entail, or me?'

Cory bristled; she couldn't help it. He was such a *know-all*; he thought he had her taped down to the last thought, she told herself crossly, and it didn't help that in this particular case he was right. But she would rather walk on coals of fire than admit it.

She drew herself up to her full five feet five, although with Max being nearly a foot taller it really didn't make much difference to the overall state of things, and stared up into his dark face. The confrontation was ridiculously like an angry little domestic tabby cat taking on one of its wild African cousins, but the analogy didn't occur to Cory until much later. 'Neither,' she lied again, her green eyes very steady. 'Why? Should I be?'

'So fierce.' It was a soft murmur, and the deep velvet note in his husky voice was so at odds with his normal curt tone that it made her knees want to buckle. 'Who, or what, has made you so prickly, Cory?' he asked as she took a step backwards away from him.

'Prickly?' It hurt; it really did. She had always regarded herself as well-balanced and generous of spirit. True, she could be fiery and emotional on occasion—she had always blamed that side of her personality on her mother's volatile genes—but she would hate to be labelled as touchy. She certainly hadn't been before she had met Max Hunter anyway, she justified quickly in the next instant. 'I'm not in the least prickly,' she stated sharply, her tone making the words a contradiction that was not lost on the man looking down at her. 'I'm not!'

'Of course you are not,' he agreed with dry sarcasm.

She had the amazing urge to stamp her foot at him—something she hadn't done since the tantrums of childhood—and checked it immediately, instead drawing on every scrap of composure and saying icily, 'I thought we had to get to the Katchui building?'

'All in good time,' he returned easily, with a coolness Cory found more than a little annoying. 'The car is coming for us in an hour; I thought we could have a cup of coffee downstairs first while we go over some of the facts and figures on that electro-ceramic report.' He raised his eyebrows questioningly, his eyes mocking.

'Fine.' She nodded quickly. The anonymity of a coffee lounge would suit her just *fine*. Anything was better than the intimacy of her hotel room. *Intimacy?* The word made her blush which in turn fuelled her irritation at herself. How was it her mind always seemed to turn in one direction with this man? She wasn't promiscuous for goodness' sake; in fact she had always tended to find the somewhat fumbling attentions from the males in her life to date definitely overrated, and had been quite happy to stop them before things got out of hand. Mind you, she *had* thought she was saving herself for Vivian. Saving herself... The term was as old-fashioned as she was, she thought with a touch of bitterness. Vivian must have had a good laugh or two at her expense in the past, and no doubt Max Hunter would split his sides if he knew he was looking at that rare oddity—a twenty-four-year-old virgin.

'Cory, I don't want to labour the point, and far be it from me to state the obvious, but I am *not* your enemy,' Max said coolly.

She had actually brushed past him and reached the half-open door when Max spoke, and when his hands touched her slender shoulders, moving her around to face him, she steeled herself to show no reaction whatsoever. 'I know that.' She tried to be very controlled and Gillianish but it wasn't easy. 'Of course I know that.'

'We are here on business,' he continued quietly, his eyes narrowed on her hot face, 'but if you are going to be so tense and on edge the whole week you'll run yourself ragged. I've great faith in you, okay? Take it as read. There will be nothing in the next few days you can't handle. Trust me.'

Oh, the irony of it. There was one six-foot-four thing she was beginning to think she was never going to be able to cope with. She had hoped, *desperately*, in the last six weeks that she would start to master this crazy see-saw of emotion that had started the first time she had ever laid eyes on Max Hunter, but it was getting worse if anything. But she'd rather die than let him know.

'I hope so.' Cory managed a fairly positive smile and was rewarded by a crooked grin that spoke of approval.

'I know so. Now...' He pushed her through the doorway and walked out after her, closing the door behind him. 'Plenty of black coffee first, I think—it wouldn't do for either of us to fall asleep on Mr Katchui, would it?—and then we'll go over a few matters before the car

comes.' He had metamorphosed into successful
tycoon again—even his voice was different—
but Cory was more than happy to go along with
the transition. Max Hunter, powerful mogul and
multimillionaire she could cope with, but Max
Hunter the man? That was where things got
sticky.

In spite of her misgivings, Cory found she coped
more than adequately with all that was expected
of her. The drive to the Katchui building was an
experience in itself. Most Japanese city roads,
streets, lanes and avenues had no names, and
those of Tokyo were no exception, but their
host's driver knew exactly where to go in the
vast maze and seemed determined to get there
at great speed.

Max further impressed her when they arrived
at Nagatacho. He seemed to understand perfectly the subtle matter of how deeply to bow
according to age and status and other delicate
matters, guiding her through the meeting and so-
cial intercourse tactfully and without any awk-
wardness so all was smoothness and nicely oiled
wheels.

Mr Katchui and his personal assistant, a
young man, both spoke good English and were
charming, insisting the four of them eat out at a

restaurant rather than allowing Max and herself to go back to the hotel once the day's business was concluded. The small but expensive restaurant specialised in the refined cuisine of kaiseki ryori, and the many small dishes of seasonal delicacies were mouthwateringly delicious, but by now Cory was so exhausted she could have been eating sawdust. But she smiled and nodded and kept up her end of the conversation as though she were as fresh as a daisy, until her cheek muscles ached and her head was thumping.

The three men had been drinking sake all night but Cory had opted for soda-water. Nevertheless, as they left the restaurant just before eleven o'clock and climbed into Mr Katchui's limousine, she felt as dizzy and nauseous as if she had consumed a whole bottle of Japan's innocuous-looking but somewhat potent national liquor.

Her head was swimming on the journey back to the hotel and her limbs felt like lead but she managed to make her goodbyes to their Japanese colleagues without disgracing herself. It was as she and Max walked into the hotel that she stumbled and almost went headlong.

'Are you all right?' Max had been a step or so behind her and caught her arm immediately, then, as he glanced down into her white face and shadowed eyes, he swore softly before saying, 'I should have realised sooner; you're exhausted.'

She really was feeling very peculiar... Cory wanted to answer him, to say something light and cool and finish the evening on an upbeat note before she could collapse into bed, but although her brain knew what it needed to say her mouth just wouldn't respond. She murmured something, some rubbish by the look on Max's face, but most of her concentration was involved in willing herself not to pass out at his feet. If she could just get to her room she'd be fine.

'Sit down there a minute.' To her horror he pushed her down in one of the big comfy seats close to the lifts in Reception and then pressed her head between her knees, but she was feeling so limp and helpless she couldn't fight him in spite of the worry she was making a spectacle of herself.

She heard him bark an order at one of the staff who had come forward to see if they could assist, and the young man immediately walked over to the lifts and held one of the doors open, presumably after pressing the button for their floor.

'I'm fine...please.' As Cory made to struggle to her feet Max swore again, his tone a low growl this time, and before she knew what was what she found herself caught up in his arms and carried over to the elevator as though she weighed no more than a child.

This couldn't be happening. The thought was there, but reality was being held firmly in muscled strong arms against a powerful ribcage with the faint, intoxicatingly sexy smell of him increasing her breathless confusion. His light grey jacket had been open when he had lifted her, and now, with her hot face buried in his shoulder, she could feel the measured thump-thump-thump of his heartbeat as he walked and the warmth of his skin.

Well, she had wondered what it would be like to be in his arms… She was so tired and defenceless that she didn't even try to deny the truth. Right from that first day at the office she had wondered, the more so as she had come to appreciate the ruthless accuracy of his discernment and razor-sharp intelligence that, when added to his overwhelming physical attributes, made him so hypnotically fascinating. And he was, as the number of different female voices who called him at the office testified to. He must have a different woman for every day of the week.

The last thought didn't help in the present situation and as Cory began to wriggle a bit a curt, deep 'Keep still, woman' made her protest, as she called on all her courage and raised her head.

'I'm all right now; I'm perfectly capable of walking.'

Scathing amber eyes met embarrassed green, and as he recognised her discomfiture his own voice mellowed a fraction. 'You are not all right,' he stated impatiently, 'and I have no intention of picking you up off the floor so just relax, there's a good girl.'

'Please, Max, this is so embarrassing. I can—'

'*I mean it, Cory.*'

Said in that tone, there was no point in disputing the matter any further, but the thought of being able to relax when held in Max Hunter's arms was just plain ridiculous, Cory acknowledged weakly. His hard-boned square jaw was just two inches from her face, her left bosom was pressed against his chest in such a way that she could feel the faint roughness of body hair beneath the silk of his shirt—in fact the whole sensual magnetism of the man was increased about a thousandfold, she thought desperately. The urge to move her head just the slightest bit

and brush her lips against the deliciously
scented male chin brought her out of the rapt
contemplation of his face like nothing else could
have done, and she just hoped he couldn't sense
the trembling that had started deep in her lower
stomach.

'I said relax, Cory.' As the lift glided to a halt
and the doors brushed silently open, Max's
voice was slightly grim. 'I'm not about to take
advantage of you, if that's what's bothering you.
You're my secretary, for crying out loud. We're
here on business.'

I know, I know. It was a wail from deep
within her. She hadn't even known this man two
months and he had turned her concept of herself
and her own sensuality upside down. Thank
goodness he didn't know how she felt. She
breathed in deeply and prayed for calm. She
would die with humiliation if he ever guessed;
she'd absolutely die.

When they reached her door Cory found herself placed very gently on her feet and it wasn't
until then that she dared open her eyes again,
which had snapped tightly shut along with the
impulse to kiss him. 'Thank you.' She was
pleased with her voice; it wasn't half as fluttery
as she'd expected it to be considering the way
her insides had reduced to melted jelly.

'My pleasure.' It was very dry. 'Let me have your key.'

'There really is no need,' she said primly. 'I can manage.'

'Your key, Cory,' he rasped irritably. 'Now.'

She gave him the key, and then, when he lifted her again and carried her over to the bed after kicking the door shut, she felt herself go hot all over. Talk about hidden fantasy night!

'Right. Now I'm going to leave you in bed and I don't want you attempting to walk until you've slept off some of this exhaustion. If you can't give me your word on that I'll sit by your bed all night.'

Cory stared up at him incredulously, totally taken aback by the cool statement, her green eyes enormous and her lips falling open in a little O of amazement before she nodded bemusedly. 'I won't move.'

'Do you need to go to the bathroom before I go?' he added expressionlessly, although she knew she had caught a little glimmer of amusement deep in the golden eyes.

'You're not coming in there with me?' she asked, aghast, before she could stop herself, hot colour flooding her face the next instant.

She thought she saw the hard mouth quiver suspiciously, but he wasn't smiling when he said, his voice smooth, 'My services would take you to the door only.'

'Oh, well, I don't need to anyway,' she managed weakly, knowing her face was as red as a beetroot. Why did he always make her feel so naive and gauche? she asked herself crossly. No one else ever had.

When he nodded slowly and then bent and eased first one shoe then the other off her feet a wave of heat brought her teeth clenching, and when he sat on the edge of the bed and—taking one swollen ankle into his lap—started expertly massaging her foot Cory felt that the frissons of sensation must be frizzing her hair.

'You should have worn more sensible shoes for this afternoon,' he said disapprovingly, with a frown at her high-heeled elegant court shoes that had cost a bomb. 'A long flight like the one from England always causes problems with swelling.'

'My feet are fine.' And then, as he raised quizzical eyebrows at the swollen flesh in his wonderfully caressing fingers, she added quickly, 'Or they will be by tomorrow.' She wanted to jerk her feet away—she had never in her wildest dreams expected to be in such an achingly vulnerable situation with Max—but because she didn't trust herself or her feelings she didn't dare do anything which might arouse that incredibly astute mind to suspect that she saw him as anything other than simply her employer.

How would she react if it was Mr Stanley sitting there stroking her feet? she asked herself feverishly. The idea was so ludicrous that she found she couldn't even give it serious thought.

'I want you to sleep in late tomorrow.' He had carefully deposited one lucky little foot on to the covers and had started ministering to the other, his fingers deft and firm as they moved fluidly over the silky honey-toned skin. 'I've got a meeting at nine but I shan't need you for that, but the one at the Saito complex with Mr Katchui at three will be long and complicated, and I'd like you fresh and alert.'

'I can be fresh and alert at nine.' Cory stared at him indignantly. Would he have had to do without Gillian at the morning meeting? She doubted it very much, or that he would have suggested it.

He considered her dryly, his head to one side and his fingers still working their magic. 'I'm not criticising your efficiency,' he drawled with sardonic accuracy, his eyes gleaming like sun-touched water in the muted lighting and his face dark and shadowed. 'And I wouldn't have asked Gillian to accompany me in the morning either,' he added impassively. 'You were wondering about that, weren't you?'

'Not at all,' she lied quickly, her heart thumping. He had read her mind again and it was happening too often for comfort.

'Little liar.' He placed her foot on the covers before standing up abruptly and Cory suddenly felt quite bereft. 'You don't lie well, Cory Masters, do you know that? Unlike most of your sex.'

For an awful, heart-stopping moment she thought he had guessed how she felt, and then her heart raced on like an express train as he continued, 'I know you are anxious to prove yourself, but you wouldn't be here if I thought there was any chance that you wouldn't come up to scratch. Believe me in that,' he added, with a slanting of those big-cat eyes that told her he was speaking the truth. 'And I never make mistakes,' he added lazily.

'Never?' The arrogance was back in full force and she didn't like it but at least it swept away any heart-stirrings.

'Never,' he affirmed imperturbably.

'Lucky old you.' She hitched herself up into a sitting position, and his power over her made her voice tart as she said, 'It must be wonderful to go through life without ever having made any mistakes, unlike the rest of the human race.'

'I didn't say that I've never made any, only that I don't now,' Max said in a distant tone that indicated he wanted to finish the conversation as he began to turn to walk away.

She was aware of the unspoken command, but a burning curiosity to know just a little more about this disturbingly charismatic man made her ignore it as she said, 'Your mistakes must have been pretty catastrophic to make you so careful these days?' Her voice managed to be both light and faintly sceptical rather than inquisitive.

He surveyed her for some twenty seconds without saying a word, and then, as the silence stretched and tautened until Cory found she was holding her breath, he said slowly, and without any apparent emotion at all, 'If you call driving one innocent young woman to her death and allowing another, who was using both her sick mind and her beautiful body, to entrap you and turn black into white catastrophic, then you are probably right.'

'Wh-what? I...I don't understand,' Cory stammered helplessly, shocked to the core at the tangible bitterness that had turned the golden eyes into dark rust and was in striking contrast to the expressionless voice. 'I don't understand what you mean.'

Max stared fixedly at her for a long moment and then shook his head abruptly, his eyes clearing as he said, his voice rough, 'There is no reason why you should. Forgive me, I should not have spoken of it; it was a long time ago and is best forgotten.'

Forgotten? Cory tried to say something, to marshal some words past the whirling confusion in her mind, but the look on his face had frozen her thought processes and she was utterly at a loss.

And this state of helpless inertia was further compounded when Max remained looking down into her troubled white face for one moment more before he said, his voice dry with cynicism now, 'Like I said, forget it, Cory. We all make mistakes, like you with this Vivian guy who's given you the run-around after stringing you along for years. The worst ones are always the best in bed.'

She gasped out loud, she couldn't help it, fierce red staining her cheekbones at his audacity, and she was still searching her mind for some caustic comment to put him in his place—wherever that was—when he bent down and casually stroked a finger across the moist fullness of her bottom lip, his touch unbearably erotic, before turning abruptly and leaving the room without another word.

CHAPTER FOUR

CORY was in such a state after Max had gone
that she expected to lie awake for hours after
she had collapsed back on the pillows behind
her, but she must have fallen asleep immediately
because the next thing she knew a tentative
dawn was casting pale mauve shadows about the
room and she had awoken to the fact that she
was still fully clothed and lying on the top of
the bed, and that she was cold.

She rose gingerly, glad to find that the weakness and giddiness seemed to have vanished, un-
dressed quickly, had a brief warm shower and
brushed her teeth, and after pulling on her
nightie climbed under the covers. She was
asleep again as soon as her head touched the
pillow, curled up in a warm ball like a sleepy
little animal.

The sun was high and streaming in through
the open curtains the next time she opened her
eyes, and when she glanced at her little bedside
alarm clock she couldn't believe it was midday.
She had slept for a full twelve hours or more,
but she felt so much better for the rest, she told

herself as she flung back the covers and stretched like a small sleek cat, before padding through to the bathroom and running herself a scented bath.

She had just emerged from the bathroom—dressed in her own short white towelling bathrobe and not the hotel's cotton yukata—with her wet hair spread about her shoulders, when the knock came at the door and made her jump.

Max? She paused in the middle of the bedroom, panic catching her breath, but then as the knock came again, more impatient this time, she yanked the belt of the robe more securely round her slender waist and walked across the room, opening the door tentatively.

'Good afternoon.' It was dry and cool and very distant.

He was in business mode, utterly the cool, expressionless tycoon, and he looked absolutely drop-dead gorgeous, Cory thought weakly, her wide eyes taking in the green shirt and pale green and grey tie he had teamed with the light grey suit of the day before. He was holding the jacket slung across one broad shoulder, and his imperturbable glance didn't falter as it took in her state of undress.

But then it wouldn't, would it? Cory thought caustically. As far as Max Hunter was concerned she held as much interest as a tomato sandwich. Especially with her hair in rat's-tails and no make-up.

'Hello.' She managed a quick smile. 'I'm just getting ready; I slept late as you advised. I can be ready in ten minutes.'

'Good.' He nodded curtly. 'I just called by to say I've ordered lunch for one, if that's okay? The car is picking us up at two o'clock for the meeting so that'll give us plenty of time.'

'Right, thank you.' Cory felt very put out without knowing why and that annoyed her still more.

'So I'll call again in…' he consulted the solid gold Rolex on his left wrist '…twenty-five minutes?' he suggested coolly.

'Fine.' She didn't smile this time and her voice was as crisp as his as he turned away without another word.

This morning's meeting couldn't have gone particularly well. Once she was alone again she dried her hair quickly, her mind gnawing at the reason for Max's distinct coolness. Or perhaps it was because she hadn't been ready to go with him at nine? But he had *told* her not to, she reminded herself firmly, and she had taken him at his word. There was nothing wrong with that, was there? No, no, there wasn't. She nodded her head sharply and stared into the green eyes in the mirror for a few moments, before reminding herself she had to get a move on and be ready for when he returned.

Once her hair was dry she secured it in a clip at the back of her head and applied the minimum of make-up to her creamed face, merely a touch of honey-gold foundation, the merest suggestion of green eyeshadow and a coating of black mascara on her thick silky lashes. She dressed simply but smartly in a calf-length jade-green linen skirt—the slim fit relieved by the above-the-knee splits on either side—and a matching shirt-style short-sleeved blouse which she wore tucked in the skirt, the whole being complemented by a wide leather belt. Gold studs at her ears, high-heeled dark brown shoes in exactly the same shade as the belt, and she was ready.

Cool efficiency married with discreet femininity. She nodded to the faintly apprehensive reflection in the mirror at the same time as Max's authoritative knock sounded at her door. She would never give him any reason to think she was trying to make him notice her, she told herself firmly as she turned to answer the door. And the sexy little black dress she had brought along—just in case—was certainly not going to emerge from the wardrobe. She was quite content for him to see her as an extension of the office—more than content. She just wished it weren't accomplished with such ease.

He was lounging against the far wall in the corridor when Cory opened the door, and in spite of the stern pep-talk she had given herself when she was getting ready Cory's heart missed a beat or two as he levered his big body straight, raking back his hair lazily.

'I'm starving,' she said brightly, her tone determinedly cheerful.

'So am I.' He seemed to have found his normal cool equilibrium, so, whatever the difficulties of the morning, Cory assumed he had settled them in his mind as he added, his eyes narrowed, 'You look cucumber-cool and very English with your clothes on. Quite different to the Aphrodite of half an hour ago.'

Aphrodite her foot! She'd left him cold. Cory smiled politely but said nothing as she shut the door and walked with him to the lifts.

They ate a light lunch and were sitting waiting in Reception some time before two o'clock, but although Max had kept the conversation flowing in his own smooth inimitable way Cory found herself wondering what he was really thinking several times as she caught the clear golden gaze.

He was an enigma. As Mr Katchui's car drew up outside the building and they rose, the thought was at the forefront of Cory's mind. Which was part of his subtle magnetism to the opposite sex, she supposed. But it was more than that; she couldn't imagine Max ever being small-minded or petty. Ruthless certainly, manipulative—when occasion warranted it—maybe, but he had been right last night when he'd said Vivian had given her the run-around, and she couldn't imagine Max Hunter stooping to such tactics to wriggle out of a commitment. Whatever Max was, he wasn't a wimp.

Was she saying Vivian was a wimp? Her eyes narrowed in the bright sunlight outside, but as she slid into the back of the limousine her mind was still worrying at the thought, and when the answer came it made her green eyes open wide. Yes, he was a wimp. She relaxed back into the seat in surprise. He had always been one; she just hadn't acknowledged it before, even through all the years of looking after him and nurturing him along. Her love for Vivian had been—she searched for the right words and found them—almost brotherly at heart, that was it. He'd been the younger brother she'd never had.

She gazed out of the window without seeing a thing. How could she have got it so wrong? she asked herself faintly. What did that make her? All the years of imagining he was the one for her, the tears and heartache when he met Carole, and now she was actually grateful for what she had to admit was a lucky escape. It would seem she knew herself even less than she had known the real Vivian.

'…if you'd like that?'

'I'm sorry?' She came back to the real world and the realisation that Max had been speaking to her and she hadn't heard a word, and now her face was flushed as she said quickly, 'I was daydreaming.'

'Right.' His voice was terse; he clearly didn't have too many women daydream in his presence. 'I asked you if you would like to visit a Japanese inn with me tonight that one of my colleagues has recommended; it's a taste of the real Japan and very different to the big western-style hotels.'

'Oh.' She blinked at him in surprise. 'Yes, thank you, that would be lovely,' she added hastily. 'I'd like that.'

'Tokyo is a long way to come without taking advantage of a little local colour,' Max said evenly as he looked into her heart-shaped face, 'and our itinerary is such that the rest of the trip is virtually programmed hour by hour, so the few hours available tonight is the only chance to have our minds broadened.'

Cory nodded again. He didn't have to spell it out, she told herself silently; she had never for one moment imagined that his invitation was in any way a date.

The meeting at the Saito plant went very well but it was still almost seven o'clock by the time things wound up. Max refused the offer of Mr Katchui's car and chauffeur for the evening and instead the two of them travelled by taxi to Akasaka in the south-west of the city. Max's colleague had given him a map with their destination clearly marked—essential in a city where building numbers generally related to the order of construction, not to position, and even the taxi drivers could rarely find anything but a big hotel, station or landmark from the address alone—and they reached the ryokan, Japanese inn, without too much trouble—a minor miracle in labyrinthine Tokyo.

'Am I dressed all right?' Cory was beginning to appreciate the hundred and one rituals that made up Japanese society, and as the taxi roared off down the narrow street, narrowly missing an old man in a cotton kimono who was clack-clacking his way home in wooden sandals, she knew a moment's panic as she stared at the attractive building in front of her. She wouldn't want to offend anyone.

'You're perfect.' As she glanced up into Max's face her stomach muscles tightened, but then he blinked and smiled, his gaze becoming almost remote, and she knew she had imagined the warmth in the golden eyes. 'And I'm hungry,' he added coolly. 'Come along.'

A path of flat rounded stepping-stones led through a pretty green garden complete with a small pool and floating water lilies, and into a neat stone-floored vestibule where a small and very beautiful middle-aged woman in a kimono was waiting. Max had telephoned the expected time of their arrival from the Saito complex, and now, as the woman smilingly indicated two pairs of slippers—one large, one small—Cory followed Max's lead and slipped off her shoes to replace them with the slippers.

Cory wasn't sure what she had been expecting—in fact the afternoon had been so gruelling and hectic she hadn't really had time to think about the evening at all—but as she and Max followed their host into the inn she was struck by the peaceful and next-to-nature ambience that the Japanese sought to create in their crowded land.

The room they were shown into was appealing in its aesthetic simplicity but small, and it was immediately clear it was not a dining room, although when Max shed his slippers before stepping through the open paper door Cory followed suit. The floor was of tatami mats, rice straw covered with finely woven reeds, the ceiling wood and the central table surrounded by floor cushions on which, Cory presumed, one sat to eat. It was uncluttered and beautiful—and intimate. Very, very intimate. And very different from a crowded western-style hotel.

'I don't understand.' Cory glanced up from her contemplation of the surroundings to find Max's gaze on her bewildered face. 'We aren't eating in here, are we?' Perhaps it was the custom that one waited in a room like this one until their table was ready? she asked herself as the butterflies in her stomach went wild. 'Where's the dining room?' she asked as steadily as she could.

'There is no dining room in a ryokan,' Max said quietly. 'All meals are served in the resident's individual rooms. Why? Is that a problem?' he added silkily.

Was it a problem? *Was it a problem!* He expected her to virtually lie on the floor with him in this romantic idyll and share a cosy little meal for two, and he asked her if it was a problem? A predicament of colossal proportions, more like. 'No, not at all.' She managed a bright smile she was proud of. 'I just wasn't expecting it, that's all. It's very...Japanese.'

'Very,' he agreed solemnly, 'and rest assured that in spite of the bedding in the cupboards beyond yon paper door—' he pointed to a far corner where paper on rectangular patterned frames of thin woodwork in the form of sliding doors were '—we *are* here just for dinner, in case you're wondering.'

'I wasn't.' It was true—Max Hunter, controlled, cold king of his emotions and the world in general interested in a little nobody like her, even for a brief interlude? No way.

'You'll never go to heaven,' he drawled lazily, crossing his arms and staring at her flushed face with something akin to amusement.

The fragile, delicate room with its low doorway—through which Max had had to bend almost double as they had entered, Japanese inns and houses not being set up for a big six-foot-four westerner—and the pale light surroundings magnified the brooding quality of his dark maleness, and for a moment Cory was tempted to let him think what he liked, but she couldn't. 'No, I really wasn't.' She faced him determinedly, looking straight into his eyes without flinching. 'It didn't occur to me you'd try anything of that nature.'

'No?' He couldn't doubt she meant what she said, and she saw a frown brush his chiselled features before he searched her hot face. 'I don't know whether to take that as a compliment or an insult,' he said with a touch of acidity that suggested he was inclined towards the latter.

'Oh, no, I didn't mean it like that,' Cory said hastily. 'I know you like women! I mean, I'm sure your sex life... I didn't think—' She broke off, aware she was digging a hole for herself and Australia was already in view. 'I didn't mean it like that...'

'So we've agreed I'm a normal red-blooded male with my fair share of hormones,' Max said smoothly without taking his eyes off her hunted face. 'In that case why would it be so unthinkable that I might have less than pure thoughts for this evening?'

How on earth had she got herself into this? Cory stared at him without speaking for a moment or two, utterly at a loss to explain herself. Her heart was beating so hard it was threatening to jump out of her chest, and he must have sensed her agitation because he gestured towards one of the cushions, his voice soft as he said, 'Sit down before you fall down, woman. I'm not trying to pick a fight,' just as the door slid open again and the maid entered with their sake, Japanese rice wine, in a vase-like bottle standing in a bowl of warm water, and steaming handtowels in small wicker baskets.

As Max joined her on the floor, his big body amazingly adept at dealing with the intricacies of the Japanese style of eating, he said quietly, 'After wiping your fingers roll the towel up again and keep it for use as a napkin.'

Cory nodded, feeing desperately uncomfortable at her lack of knowledge of the country's customs in front of the exquisite little maid, and it was this feeling that prompted her to say, before she considered her words, 'We *are* going to eat alone, aren't we?' The smiling woman served them the sake in tiny glasses—no bigger than eggcups—and solicitously knelt at their side.

'You'd prefer that?' Max asked softly, his eyes glittering.

'I think so. I know so little about Japanese etiquette and so on, I wouldn't like to offend...'

'You wouldn't offend, Cory.' His voice was warm and as she blinked and looked at him he added, 'But if you'd be more comfortable...'

He spoke to the maid in rapid Japanese and she rose gracefully, bowing prettily before she left, but now Cory was regretting the fact that her hasty words had placed them in a more intimate position than if a third party had been present. He wouldn't think... She glanced at him from under her eyelashes as he refilled her glass with the fifteen per cent alcohol that tasted like delicious dry sherry. No, of course he wouldn't, she reassured herself in the next instant. She had never given him the slightest sign of a come-on, just the opposite in fact, and he found her as attractive as a block of wood.

'Now...' Max surveyed her easily from his position just inches away, and the fact that he had discarded his jacket and his tie and undone the first few buttons of his shirt was not helping her breathing, she acknowledged silently as she surreptitiously took another fortifying glass of sake. 'Where were we? Oh, yes, you were about to tell me why it would be so inconceivable that I might have ulterior motives for this little sojourn out of life's hectic rat race.'

He was enjoying this. As Cory stared into the dark male face she found she was angry. Angry at the position he had placed her in in pressing the issue, angry at his comfortable male arrogance and sureness that he was in control, but more than that—much more than that—she was angry at the fact that however much she tried to fight it she found this man so darned *attractive*. It was pure stupidity—and his morals, his lifestyle, his attitude to women was everything she disliked—but physically... Physically...

The adrenalin pumping round her body—along with the sake—enabled her voice to be both reasonable and cool as she played him at his own game. 'Because you are my employer of course,' she said with wide-eyed innocence, 'and naturally you are aware I could never look on you as anything other than a business colleague. That is the essence of all successful work relationships, isn't it?'

He listened without moving a muscle but nevertheless she had the feeling that his whole body had stiffened, and his stillness was further emphasised when she continued blithely, even managing a comradely smile, 'And of course you are an experienced man of the world, you've been around a lot longer than I have, and I'm sure your world is as different to mine as chalk to cheese. We've nothing in common, absolutely nothing—beyond work, that is—and although it might not be sophisticated to say so I could never indulge in the sort of casual affair that city folk seem to find so acceptable. My ''cloud-cuckoo'' mentality wouldn't let me,' she finished sweetly.

There was a long pause—a really long pause—where the air fairly crackled with electricity, and then she saw him take a deep pull of air. 'Quite.' It was smooth and silky and covered sharp steel and the mocking arrogance had quite gone.

If you can't stand the heat, don't come into the kitchen. It was one of her mother's favourite barbs but it fitted perfectly. She might be a little hillbilly from the wilds of Yorkshire in his eyes, Cory told herself with a touch of bitterness, as his comments the day before had made perfectly clear, but she had a mind of her own and she wasn't afraid to use it. How *dared* he laugh at her and treat her like some pet poodle? And that was what it had boiled down to. And she wasn't having it!

'More sake?' He refilled her glass and Cory swigged it with something of a 'what the hell' bravura, ignoring the fact that she hadn't eaten for some seven or so hours.

The meal, when it came, was very good. The seafood morsels, dipped in a light batter and cooked very quickly in boiling oil, were crisply delicious; the soup—drunk from the bowl as if it were a cup with the vegetables picked out with chopsticks—was subtle in flavour, and the rice and palate-fresheners and other dishes were all superb in their own right.

Max taught her that the slurping of the soup and noodles was a sign that the dish was being properly savoured, that rice was usually eaten by holding the bowl close to the mouth and using chopsticks—no mean feat in itself, Cory discovered as she shovelled the rice in—and that warm sake in between mouthfuls was wonderfully beneficial, if not actually etiquette in the strictest sense.

They were well on their way to consuming the second bottle of sake when Cory became aware of the warm sense of euphoria that was enveloping her like a rich blanket. She was comfortably replete, and in the last few minutes all the petty irritations, along with the pain and confusion of the last twelve months, had simply melted away.

Somehow, in the last half an hour or so, Max had drawn closer and now her shoulder was resting against his, but it seemed like the height of bad manners to move away. The height of bad manners... What sort of woman did he prefer? She contemplated him lazily from under her eyelashes as she finished her umpteenth eggcup of sake. Cool, sophisticated blondes? Voluptuous, warm brunettes? Volatile, fiery redheads? Probably all of them, she thought grumpily.

Gillian had told her that he had girlfriends—lots of girlfriends—but that none of them lasted more than a few months at most, and they all knew the score. 'He treats them well, spoils them rotten,' Gillian had said with a sightly disapproving edge to her voice, 'and then says goodbye with charm and generosity while everything is still sweet. It's Max's way.'

'Don't they mind?' she'd asked Gillian in astonishment.

'Max chooses like for like,' Gillian had said quietly. 'He doesn't want emotional involvement and neither do his women. His lifestyle is fast and wild and he works hard and plays hard. He puts all his commitment and energy into Hunter Operations; when he wants to relax he wants fun without any ties or obligations. That's how he is. That's Max—he makes it clear he can take it or leave it.'

Gillian had changed the subject then, as though regretting that she had said too much, but Cory had felt there was more unsaid than said. And after the disturbing conversation she had had with Max the night before she felt it all tied in with this catastrophic 'mistake' he had spoken of, which still clearly affected him very much although he would deny it. What had happened? The thought had been there in the back of her mind, nagging away all day. He couldn't really have been responsible for someone dying...could he?

'That was a wonderful meal.' Probably due to the nature of her thoughts Cory decided the silence was becoming uncomfortable and that she had to break it. Max, on the other hand, had been stretched out in apparent relaxation at the side of her, the slumberous dark attraction that he exuded as naturally as breathing emphasised by his lazy contentment and the delicate, almost feminine surroundings.

'Wasn't it,' he agreed softly, turning his head and letting his eyes stroke over her face as he spoke. 'Delicious...'

'What's that noise?' Cory had been conscious of a plaintive and somewhat poignant sound for the last few minutes, something far removed from everyday life and almost fairylike, which perfectly fitted this step out of reality. 'I've never heard it before.'

'It's a soba seller, a street vendor of noodles,' Max said quietly. 'He announces his presence through the streets by blowing his tin flute to attract customers. It's a melancholy sound but one which everyone recognises.'

He had slightly shifted his position as he spoke and Cory, anxious to put some space between them, seized the opportunity to sit up straighter but in so doing caught the clip holding her thick coil of hair. As the clasp sprung loose and her hair fell about her face and shoulders in a soft veil of shimmering silk she made a faint sound of distress, reaching for the clip which had jumped under the table.

'Don't.' As her fingers reached the clasp Max's hand covered hers. 'Leave it.' Cory tensed, holding her breath until he leant back again and said, his voice wry with self-mockery, 'I've been wondering what your hair looks like loose for six weeks and now I know. It's criminal to hide such beauty.'

'I prefer to be tidy and neat for the office,' Cory protested as primly as the semi-reclining position and his dark presence would allow. 'Long hair would get in the way.'

'We aren't in the office now,' he said softly, his voice husky.

She was painfully aware that something had shifted and changed in the last minute or so, something indefinable but nevertheless very potent. Something that was making shivers trickle down her spine.

She knew he was going to kiss her, and she also knew it would be the height of foolishness to allow him to do so, but as she stared into his gold eyes which were coming closer—her green gaze wide and mesmerised like a small cat caught frozen in the powerful amber lights of an oncoming car—she waited for his mouth to touch hers with a breathless hunger that was paralysing.

His lips were warm and searching at first and he made no move to hold her or draw her into him as the kiss deepened. She had known he would be able to kiss—the sensual expertise was evident in every movement and glance he made, even the way he carried the big male body with such confidence and authority—but she had never guessed a kiss could hold such mind-blowing sovereignty as this one. He knew just how to entice, to please, and he wasn't even *touching* her apart from his mouth on hers, she told herself swimmingly as a million and one nerve-endings became sensitised into one aching whole.

So this is what those other women enjoyed, she thought helplessly. But how, having once experienced Max Hunter making love to them, could they ever be content with any other man?

And then, her eyes shut, she ceased to think, abandoning herself to the eroticism of the sensations he was arousing in her. When she felt herself moulded into the strong male body it didn't even occur to her to object; she was fluid and felt molten heat as his lips moved to her ears, the hollow of her throat and then lower.

'So beautiful...' He was murmuring huskily in between the burning kisses. 'Your skin is translucent, do you know that? I've never seen such delicacy before, and your hair... Spun silk.'

Cory had lost all idea of time, along with every scrap of common sense she had ever possessed. She was in another sphere, a new dimension, where touch and taste and smell were heightened to an unbearable intensity and all that mattered was his lips and hands and what they were doing to her.

He was kissing her mouth again, passionately and intoxicatingly, fiercely, parting her lips with a dominant authority she didn't even try to resist, but the sensuality was exquisitely controlled too—even though his heart was beating like a sledgehammer against the softness of her breasts he wasn't trying to force her or go too quickly. It was heady, wonderful, and she couldn't get enough of it.

Her hands were on the broad thrust of his muscled shoulders and he was exploring her mouth in such a way that she was unable to disguise the shivers fluttering down her spine, the skilful plundering rendering her exposed and defenceless. His hands were caressing her body with a dexterity and knowledge that sent waves of desire coursing through her veins, and she found herself longing for his touch on her bare skin, their clothing a barrier that brought frustrated little moans deep within her throat. She hadn't imagined she could feel like this. She hadn't known...

Quite when she became aware that he was merely holding her—his mouth restrained as he brushed gentle little kisses on her forehead— Cory wasn't sure, but with the knowledge came a deep and humiliating awareness of just how completely she had submitted to him, the sounds of her own little inarticulate cries still echoing in her ears and her breathing uneven and ragged.

'Cory, I'm sorry; I shouldn't have done that.'

She couldn't believe what he was saying for a moment—that he had actually *stopped*—and then as she pulled away she was free immediately, Max's hands making no effort to hold her.

If she had glanced at him in that moment she would have seen a confusion and darkness in the beautiful slanted eyes that might have gone some way to alleviating her own embarrassment. As it was she fumbled with her clothes for some seconds before looking at him, and it was an imperturbable cold mask that stared back, and his voice was cool as he repeated, 'I shouldn't have done that; there's no excuse beyond the magic of this place.'

How did she handle this? She wanted to die with shame and mortification at his easy mastery over her, to scream at him that he was every low name she could think of and that she loathed and detested him, but that would only make matters worse. The facts were that he had leant across and kissed her and her response to that gesture had sent things escalating out of control, Cory thought wretchedly. She should have allowed his lips to rest on hers for a few moments and then pulled back with some light, easy comment that would have kept things on an even keel. He had *told* her the last thing he wanted was for his secretary to have any romantic notions about him; he'd dotted the i's and crossed the t's early on in that respect. He was a sophisticated man of the world—a kiss meant nothing at all to such men—and she'd practically *eaten* him.

She drew on all her resources and managed a smile that, if a little shaky round the edges, was the best she could do. 'The magic of the place and the sake,' she said as lightly as she could. 'The effect of it creeps up on you, doesn't it?' She had never felt so stone-cold sober in her life. 'I wouldn't have indulged quite so freely if I'd known,' she added, with another attempt at a smile.

'It's deceptive,' he agreed easily, and she hated him for the apparent effortless control. Here was she, feeling like something the cat had dragged in with her mind blown to smithereens, and the rat wasn't even hot under the collar, she told herself bitterly. How *could* she have been so incredibly, wantonly stupid?

They remained at the inn for another twenty minutes or so, which took on the torture of twenty hours as far as Cory was concerned. She didn't dare try to put her hair up—her hands were trembling so much she knew she would be all fingers and thumbs, and the last thing she needed was further humiliation—and if their little maid noticed it when she came to collect the dishes she gave no indication.

Max was his normal smooth and urbane self on the drive back to the hotel and Cory struggled to meet him halfway and keep her end of the conversation going, but it was difficult. Every fibre of her being seemed determined to recall how it had felt to be in his arms, the taste of his mouth on hers, the enveloping warm male smell of him that was the blend of his unique aftershave and his own bodily chemicals.

She knew the kiss had meant nothing to him, that it had been dismissed as a mistake the second he had let her go and as such disqualified from further thought. Max Hunter would never waste time on anything unimportant, she told herself bitterly as the taxi hurtled towards their hotel in the rainbows of light that was Tokyo at night, when ten thousand restaurants and drinking dens beckoned with flashing signs and glowing lanterns.

He was a cold, unfeeling monster! She risked a sidelong glance at him and saw the hard, strong face was perfectly calm and relaxed. She couldn't imagine any woman wanting to get involved with him, she really couldn't, whether they were of the same icy temperament as him or not. Thank goodness, *thank goodness* he had stopped before any harm was done. They'd just shared a kiss, that was all, just a kiss, and if nothing else it had awakened her to just what sort of a man he really was. She was glad this had happened; *she was*. In the long run it was probably the best thing.

The recriminations against both herself and Max and the downright lies continued to fortify her until they had said goodnight—a cool and very swift goodnight—outside her door, and Cory found herself in the sanctuary of her hotel room.

She sat on her bed without moving or making any effort to undress for a good ten minutes, her mind going over every word, every glance, every caress they had shared until she collapsed back against her pillows with a despairing little sigh. What a mess. What a twenty-four-carat mess. He had been aroused back there at the ryokan. The memory of his body, taut and hungry, pressed against hers brought hot colour into her cheeks. But then what man wouldn't be when it was virtually being offered to him on a plate?

No. No, she hadn't been that bad…had she? No, she hadn't. She nodded to herself abruptly as she rose up from the bed. And although he might have been surprised at her reaction to what he'd probably meant as no more than a brief peck, a man of his experience should have pulled back before things went so far. It wasn't *all* her fault. This time the nod was even more determined.

She padded through to the *en suite*, discarding her clothes on the way, and ran herself a warm bath, staying in the perfumed water until it was quite cold, after which she washed her hair and then wrapped herself in her towelling bathrobe.

Tonight had been a lesson she wouldn't forget. She stared at the anxious-eyed reflection in the mirror for a full minute, worrying at her bottom lip with small white teeth. But it had happened and she couldn't do anything about it now except learn from it. She would never, *ever* allow Max Hunter to kiss her again—not that he would be foolish enough to try after tonight, no doubt. But she wouldn't anyway. It might take a few days but then all this would become history and she could forget the humiliating part and just look on it as another thread in life's rich tapestry.

She shut her eyes tightly, opening them and seeing the ridiculousness of her declaration in the cloudy green gaze staring back at her. Forget it? How could she forget it? That kiss, everything that followed had been the most devastating experience of her entire life, and he had dismissed it as easily as blowing his nose! She wished she had never taken the job as his secretary. Tears were pricking behind the backs of her eyes and she blinked them away fiercely. But she had and she would make a success of it now even if it killed her.

CHAPTER FIVE

CORY got ready to go down to breakfast the next morning after a very careful make-up session aimed at hiding the ravages of a sleepless night. She had tossed and turned until gone three and then given up all thoughts of sleep, and rather than wasting the time doing endless post-mortems on the evening with Max had made a conscious decision to get immersed in work. She'd tidied up all her notes on her laptop computer, typed out two reports she thought might be relevant for Max for the day ahead, and generally got together all the facts and figures they had discussed with Mr Katchui and the others so far.

At six o'clock she had a shower and lay down on the bed for an hour to compose herself for the day ahead, and at seven rose and began getting dressed. She tried on every item of clothing she'd brought with her over the next half an hour—apart from the sexy little black dress—and, once she had discarded them all, repeated the procedure until she was thoroughly confused and over-warm.

She wanted to look cool, collected, self-assured and competent. But feminine. Feminine and attractive. And *definitely* not desperate for a man—or, to be more precise, Max Hunter. And from her response to his kiss he might be thinking just that.

She wriggled in front of the mirror, sighed deeply, and cast an eye over the heap of clothes on the bed. Oh, this was ridiculous! She grabbed an armful and replaced them in the wardrobe with savage haste, before dressing in a simple grey skirt and white blouse teamed with plain white high heels and white daisy earrings. Very secretarialish and restrained. It would do.

Discreet make-up had hidden the mauve shadows under her eyes and she fastened her hair in a neat, authoritative French pleat with no-nonsense firmness, ignoring the echo of his words the night before.

She was ready. She glanced at her watch and saw there were ten minutes to go before half past eight—the time she had arranged to eat breakfast with Max. Should she go down and be already seated when he made an appearance? He would no doubt knock on her door on his way to the dining room if she remained here, and perhaps it would be better to face him in a crowded room than in a deserted corridor? She nodded at the thought, her heart thumping crazily. Yes, that was what she'd do. Decision made, she couldn't grab her bag quick enough, and as she opened the door in a nervous flurry she was overwhelmingly relieved the corridor was empty.

And so it was that Cory was seated at a table for two, sipping at a small glass of fresh orange juice and nibbling on a slice of toast, when Max strode into the dining room some five minutes later.

She raised a cool, secretarial hand at his entrance and once he reached her side she was proud of the distant smile and her steady, 'Good morning, Max. I trust you slept well?' as she glanced at him.

'Fine, thanks.'

Yes, he looked like he had, Cory thought venomously. The dark tanned face was smiling and relaxed, the big body dressed as immaculately as always, and he just *exuded* tranquillity and self-control. She loathed him. She did, she *loathed* him. 'Good.' She forced the smile a kilowatt or two brighter.

'And you?' he asked easily as a waiter appeared at his side.

'Like a top, thanks,' she answered smartly.

Once the attentive waiter had taken Max's order, Cory indicated the folder on the table. 'I thought it might be an idea to put some facts and figures on paper, so I jotted down a few things before I came down to breakfast.' Well, it wasn't a lie. Three in the morning *was* before breakfast. 'Here.' She handed him the two reports as she spoke, and then busied herself pouring two cups of coffee, glad to give her hands something to do and her eyes something to focus on other than Max's face.

'Excellent.' The amber gaze flashed over the neatly printed columns before raising itself to her face.

Yes, they are excellent, you hard, unfeeling swine.

It was a thought that stayed with her for the rest of the day—or the hard, unfeeling swine part of it at least—and by the time they returned to the hotel for dinner Cory felt like a piece of limp lettuce—good for nothing.

Nevertheless, she determinedly prepared for dinner as though it was an important manoeuvre in a military campaign—which wasn't far from the truth—and after a warm shower and a change of clothes she sailed downstairs with Max for cocktails as though she hadn't a care in the world, bright and sparkling and as fresh as a daisy.

By the time he returned her to her room at just gone ten o'clock she was working purely on automatic again, but at least the long, exhausting day, followed by an even more exhausting couple of hours in Max's company over dinner, made sure she fell asleep that night as soon as her head touched the pillow.

And so it was for the next few days. Cory aimed to be the perfect efficient machine Max expected of his secretary-cum-personal assistant, and Max was his usual cool, controlled self. He hadn't once mentioned the evening in the ryokan, and Cory would rather be hung, drawn and quartered than bring it up herself.

She found the days quite easy to handle as it happened. Max Hunter, demanding, dynamic tycoon and human whirlwind, was one thing, but the evenings... The evenings were a different matter. He quite naturally slipped into the mode of attentive dinner companion then, and despite all the pep-talks she gave herself in the privacy of her room his particular brand of lethal sex appeal just tied her up in knots each night. Which was *so* pathetic...

He was perfectly correct of course. In fact everything he did and said made it clear he was treating her in exactly the same way he would treat any woman—from the age of seventeen to seventy—who had been forced on him by necessity. He was charming, polite, amusing and courteous, but each night she fell under that dark magnetism a little more. And resented it a little more too.

By the time their last morning in Japan dawned, Cory was just about on her knees— figuratively speaking. Throughout the protracted goodbyes with Mr Katchui and others she smiled until her face ached, made all the right noises and said all the right things. Mr Katchui had liked her, she'd sensed that, but she was still very surprised and touched when the hard Japanese businessman gave her a small gift on parting, along with a good deal of flowery compliments.

'You made a real hit there.'

Max's tone was appreciative as they sped through Tokyo's streets towards the airport, and she smiled briefly before saying, 'It was very kind of him to give me something; I didn't expect it.'

'Open it.' He gestured at the small gift-wrapped package on her lap, his tawny eyes stroking over her face for a moment.

'Oh, it's lovely…' The little box contained a tiny figure of Hachiko, the dog in the story, which had been worked in fine silver and was quite exquisite in its own way. The small accompanying note was simple: 'Faithfulness should always be rewarded.'

Cory wasn't quite sure if she liked being compared to a female dog, but she took the compliment in the spirit in which it had been made as she showed the card to Max. 'Isn't that sweet?'

'Do I sense a message in there for me?' he asked dryly.

'Oh, I'm sure not,' Cory answered quickly. The close confines of the taxi were a little too close for her comfort—the waves of dark sex appeal were flowing hot and strong.

'Hmm, I wonder.' He eyed her somewhat morosely for a moment before he said, his voice tinged with something she couldn't quite place, 'And do you agree with that noble sentiment, Cory?'

'That faithfulness should be rewarded?' she asked carefully. 'Well, in a perfect world that would be very nice, but it doesn't always work out like that, does it?'

'Indeed it doesn't.' It was a little too abrupt— there was a raw nerve showing somewhere—

and her face must have shown her surprise because in the next instant she saw Max make a visible effort to relax, and his voice was less caustic as he said, 'I'm sorry, it's just that I let someone down badly once and I learnt there's not always time to make amends. That's all.'

'Right.' It wasn't a question of 'that's all' by the look on his face, Cory thought bemusedly, and she found her heart was racing at the sudden glimpse of the real Max Hunter. His eyes were dark again, and there was the same look in them she had seen once before, that night in her hotel room when he had spoken of this young woman he had supposedly driven to her death. 'Well, we all make mistakes.' Trite—too trite, she thought helplessly, but she couldn't think of anything else.

'That we all do.'

Now his tone was both mocking and patronising and it caused her to say, as she fired back without really thinking, 'I'm sorry, Max, I didn't aim to be flippant but I'm sure you would prefer that to me asking questions? You're not exactly easy to talk to at the best of times.' Conversation with him was more like walking through a minefield.

'Aren't I?' He shifted in his seat as he spoke, turning to face her head-on, and she saw, to her secret amusement, that she had really offended him. He was so used to any woman he was with giving unconditional homage to anything he did or said, she thought a touch astringently, that he just didn't expect any come-back. Women didn't criticise the great Max Hunter—they fell at his feet in humble adoration.

And now he backed that theory as he added brusquely, 'You're the only person who thinks so.'

'Perhaps I'm the only person who has *said* so,' Cory argued calmly, her tone sweet. She could afford to be sweet—she'd rattled him and it felt wonderfully good after the torture of the last few evenings, sitting across the table from him over dinner, and thinking he must be the most attractive man alive.

He frowned, his strong jaw squaring and his eyes narrowing to golden slits of light. The expression did incredible things to her nerves, making him, as it did, about ten times more sexy. 'Look...' He paused again, and now she found herself totally disarmed when he said in quite a different tone that sounded almost boyish, 'Do you really think I'm hard to talk to? I'm sure Gill didn't. I think we used to talk about practically everything.'

Gillian didn't fancy the pants off you. She managed a shrug but speaking was beyond her for the moment. How could one man be such a combination of hard, powerful, ruthless macho man and charming, fascinating, sexy little boy-cum-black-hearted philanderer all in one package? And how could *she* have been so stupid as to agree to work for someone she'd never seen?

He continued to survey her for one more moment as the taxi hurtled along at breakneck speed, and then his scowl cleared and it was clear he had come to some sort of a decision as he settled back in his seat again and said, very quietly, 'The person I let down was my fiancée. I was set up to believe she'd been having an affair with someone else and I didn't believe her protestations of innocence. I dumped her, very publicly, and then immediately started an affair with her sister who had always made it clear she was willing and available. Saving face, I think they call it.'

Cory stared at him, utterly appalled, before she managed to pull herself together and say fairly steadily, 'And the sister was the one who...?' She raised enquiring eyebrows.

'Set me up, yes,' Max affirmed grimly.

'How...how did you find out the truth?' Cory asked faintly.

'A couple of weeks after we broke up my fiancée drove her car into a stone wall,' Max said dispassionately, but she could see the muscle working in his jaw and sensed the iron control he was putting on himself. 'The police said it was an accident—sharp corner on a lonely country road with an old barn least where you'd expect it—but Anne knew different and she confessed all to me in a paroxysm of remorse that was as shallow as she was. Within days she'd convinced herself Laurel had really had an accident and not taken her own life and she even tried to back-pedal on what she had said.'

'She might have been right?' Cory questioned carefully.

'Laurel was an excellent driver.' It was very cool and very final. 'Anyway, within weeks my father had had his heart attack and died and I'd inherited so there was no time for further regrets.'

No further regrets? He was eaten up with them.

'What did the rest of your family think about Laurel?' Cory tried to make her voice matter-of-fact and calm but it was hard. Very hard. Surely his mother or someone had tried to comfort him?

'There was no other family besides my father,' Max said shortly. 'My mother died when I was two and I was an only child, and my father never remarried. He wasn't a family type of man anyway.'

She was further aghast but she knew Max well enough by now to know that any show of sympathy would not go down well. But never to have known his mother... But all this explained a lot, Cory thought in the next instant. To have grown up without the softening influence of a mother in his formative years and then to have his faith in the female sex shattered so cruelly—it was little wonder that he had become so cynical and disenchanted. Of course the fact that he was wealthy beyond most folks' wildest dreams and had the sort of smouldering good looks and magnetic appeal that would give any star of the silver screen a run for their money couldn't have helped. He would have had women throwing themselves at him all his life. One click of his fingers and no doubt they were lining up.

The thought pierced her through, bringing, as it did, the night in the Japanese inn into vivid clarity again. He must have thought she was just like all the rest. She *had* been like all the rest!

It brought her sitting up a little straighter and her voice was quite brisk when she said, 'Well, I admit you might have more cause than most to be a little wary of the concepts of love and faithfulness, but that doesn't make them any less a reality.'

'You're not going to go on about this village of the good and pure where you were born again, are you?' he asked with cutting sarcasm. 'Because believe me you've done it to death.'

It worked like an icy shower on the lingering compassion his previous disclosures had produced, and now Cory glared at him, her eyes ablaze with green fire as she snapped, 'Really? It couldn't just be that you hate to be proved wrong, could it? I know hundreds of couples, my own parents included, who are very happy together. I'm sorry but I don't believe they've all got it wrong.'

'Hundreds...' he drawled laconically. 'It couldn't be that *you* are exaggerating now, could it?'

'And they are *real* people,' Cory continued with blistering determination. 'People who are prepared to acknowledge their mistakes and then get on with life rather than running away.'

The cool equanimity was wiped off his face in an instant, and in the same moment Cory reminded herself that this was her boss—*her boss*—and however liberal an approach Max encouraged with his secretaries she had gone just a touch too far. But she wasn't going to back down. No way, no how. He could dismiss her for all she cared! She had as much right as he did to say what she thought.

'Running away? I take it that was meant for me?' he asked with icy dignity, his face set and cold.

Her chin went up another notch at the look in the beautiful tawny eyes. 'What would you call it?' she asked tightly. 'You said yourself you were set up by this Anne, and if anyone is prepared to lie baldly enough they can be believable. You reacted perfectly understandably in the circumstances—'

'Thank you,' he interjected with lethal sarcasm.

'And therefore, in spite of the tragic outcome, you weren't really to blame for Laurel's death. Her sister was. And it might just have been that the accident *was* an accident anyway. Whatever you say, you don't know for sure,' Cory continued doggedly as she ignored the interruption. 'You aren't God, Max.'

He stared into the violet-splashed emerald pools for a long moment before he said, his tone very cool, 'If you love someone, *really* love them shouldn't trust be a basic ingredient of that emotion? In fact shouldn't it be the foundation stone?'

Cory looked back at him, and now her voice was wary as she answered, 'Yes...' Now what was coming? she asked herself silently.

'I thought I was madly in love with Laurel—I was planning to spend the rest of my life with her, for crying out loud—but I didn't believe her when she said she wasn't involved with someone else. Oh, Anne had set up an elaborate concoction of innuendoes and lies, but that was one of the things that Laurel flung at me when she was protesting her innocence. She said if I'd loved her, *really* loved her, I would have trusted her. And she was right.'

There was more coming and Cory waited for the punch-line without saying a word, her eyes tight on his dark face.

'But I sailed in there like a gunboat with all guns firing, and do you know why? Because my pride had been hurt, that's why. And when you come down to it that's what this idealised emotion called love is all about. It doesn't exist, Cory, not really, not as we're led to believe by the poets and romantics anyway. Those couples that stay together do so because it suits them—

career-wise, or because there's children involved or because they haven't met anyone else
they fancy more—a million different reasons.'

Cory could see he meant every word and it
was in that moment, for no apparent reason, that
the thunderbolt hit. She loved him. *She loved
Max Hunter.* A man who didn't know the meaning of the word.

'And all the divorces and broken families and
the rest of it bear testimony to the validity of
what I'm saying,' Max continued evenly. 'Love
is just another name for sexual desire, physical
chemistry, but most women—and some men
too—can't engage in sex without it coming under the blanket of the name of love. They were
probably repressed emotionally when they were
young, or brainwashed, something like that,' he
added with magnificent condescension. 'It happens all the time, unfortunately.'

She didn't believe it! Cory was still too shattered by the revelation of her own stupidity to
respond to what he was saying. She'd fallen in
love with this man—this powerful, incredibly
wealthy, horribly attractive and wildly sexy
man—who had had more women than she'd had
hot dinners, and who looked for cool sophistication and unlimited sexual experience in his
women besides them being beautiful and

wealthy and gorgeous to boot. He would never look twice at someone like her, for goodness' sake.

And then, as though to prove her wrong, Max said, his voice even more bland, 'Take us for instance. I wanted you that night at the ryokan and I know you wanted me too, but it wouldn't have meant anything besides a brief satisfying of our carnal appetites, and it would certainly have interfered with our working together in the future. It shouldn't—assuaging the sexual hunger should be no more important than eating together or conversing—whatever—but the human race has been conditioned to think otherwise.'

Cory was aware she was gaping like a stranded fish, her mouth wide, and now she shut it with a little snap before forcing herself to say, her voice slightly shaky in spite of all her will being brought to bear, 'Are…are you saying you don't believe in love at all?' The subject of their wanting each other she ducked. There might be some women who could handle a live grenade but she wasn't one of them, especially when it was thrown by Max Hunter.

'Exactly.'

Cory felt an awful surge of temper at the overt self-assurance, but along with it there was a terrifying recognition of just how strong his power over her was, and it moderated her response as she said, her voice trembling, 'I don't believe that.'

'Of course you don't.' He was just plain patronising now and the anger increased. 'That's what I'm saying; you've been taught otherwise. You are a child of your environment after all.'

'I haven't been *taught* anything!' The secretarial college she had attended to get her excellent qualifications would be appalled if they could hear her now, Cory thought wretchedly as the echo of her shriek vibrated the airwaves. Screaming at one's boss was definitely a no-no. 'I'm a normal human being, for goodness' sake; it's *normal* to love! And to want to be loved,' she added more quietly. 'It's the most basic desire there is and stronger than lust.'

'I don't agree.' He eyed her coolly, quite unmoved. 'But I take it you're saying it was love, not lust you felt for Vivian?' And then, hitting way below the belt, he said, 'Now correct me if I'm wrong but I seem to remember that this great love that drove you to London, and had you all pale and wan beforehand, I'm sure, was the same love that some weeks later you weren't sure if you wanted or not.'

'What?' Cory stared at him angrily, her cheeks flushing.

'You stated you would be in two minds whether to take him back if he came crawling on bended knees,' Max stated triumphantly. 'Now, didn't you? This ''most basic desire'' can be a trifle capricious?'

How could you love someone and want to do them extreme physical damage at the same time? Cory asked herself furiously.

'And if you loved him in the way you think of love, you wouldn't have responded to me the way you did in the inn either,' he added firmly. 'You see? Love just doesn't stand up to the test.'

Oh, no, no, she could take so much and no more! The pig! The arrogant, self-satisfied, over-sexed, rotten *pig*! She called on all her considerable supply of will-power and prayed for the right words. They came. 'But you've already said that what we felt was just animal attraction,' Cory said sweetly. 'If I'd have gone to bed with you it would have just been like having a sandwich if I was hungry or going for a swim if I was too warm. It wouldn't have taken anything from Vivian because it wouldn't have mattered that much.' She clicked her fingers in his handsome supercilious face.

That face had to be seen to be believed. If anyone had told Cory she would have the satisfaction of seeing the great and imperious Max Hunter utterly lost for words she wouldn't have believed them. But it was good. Oh, it was so, *so* good.

And then the gratification was swept away and sheer alarm took its place as he said, very softly and yet with deadly intent, 'Cory, if I made love to you it wouldn't be at all like having a sandwich or going for a swim, and it would matter. Believe me, it would matter.'

She eyed him warily. He was mad. Oh, boy, was he mad!

'And if that was a challenge I'll give you something on account to convince you,' he added silkily.

He had totally ignored her squeak of panic as he had drawn closer, but stuck as she was on the back seat of a taxi there was absolutely nowhere to go. She attempted sweet reason as she quickly protested, 'It wasn't a challenge. It was you who said—'

The rest of her words were lost as his mouth took hers in a kiss that was scalding hot and shatteringly experienced, and in spite of all their previous conversations Cory went down beneath it like dry ground opening up to life-giving rain.

His mouth was hard and sensual and she would never have thought it could have produced such an instant reaction all over her body but it was happening. And Max Hunter was a man on a mission—he was making sure it was happening. She knew it, but she couldn't do a thing about it.

She could feel her breasts swelling beneath the prim, high-necked and sedately buttoned blouse she was wearing, their tender, rose-tipped peaks growing hard and aching, pressed as they were against the hard male chest. She felt dizzy, disorientated, her head swimming even as her limbs became fluid and her breathing nothing more than helpless gasps, and overall, overall was a wonderful feeling of utter pleasure that outdid anything she had experienced in her life before. He was just so *good* at this!

He had curved her into him, his body covering hers as he leant over her, and the smell of him was all about her and it was intoxicating, delicious, like all the good things in life rolled up in one package.

His hands had stroked down to her slim hips, moulding her into him so she could feel every inch of his hard arousal, and it added to her excitement. She was burning, burning all over, she thought in wonder, and they weren't even in bed. They were in a taxi heading for Narita airport in the middle of a busy weekday morning.

The same thought must have occurred to Max because in the next moment she was free and he had settled back into his own corner of the seat, surveying her through narrowed amber eyes as he said, 'Well? Now tell me the egg and cress sandwich has it.'

She would have loved to be able to fire back with a barbed retort that would have put him very firmly in his place, but Max Hunter didn't have a place, she thought helplessly. Nevertheless she straightened her blouse and skirt carefully—she wanted to tidy her hair but she knew her hands were trembling and she'd never manage the pins that were holding the French pleat in place—and kept her voice as steady as she could when she said, 'This is sexual harassment, you know that, don't you?'

'Sexual...?' His voice trailed away but only for a moment. 'Cory, grubby little has-beens go in for sexual harassment. I most definitely do not!' he stated with grim ferocity, the self-satisfied expression he had been wearing just two seconds earlier no more. 'And you enjoyed that as much as I did. Be honest, admit it.'

'Enjoying it or not enjoying it is nothing to do with it,' she snapped back with equal ferocity. 'I neither asked nor wanted you to kiss me; *that* is the point. Just who do you think you are anyway? Being mauled on the back seat of a taxi is not my idea of enjoyment, let me tell you, Max Hunter!'

The silence was profound, but as the temperature of the atmosphere between them went plummeting to below zero Cory held her ground as she stared back into the angry male face. He'd used brute force and that was unforgivable.

'I don't believe this.' It was a furious mutter, but underneath the rage was a very genuine echo of absolute bewilderment.

'I'm sure you don't.' She didn't allow herself to weaken in the slightest, and her voice was very tart. 'The trouble with you, Max Hunter, is that you've got used to snapping your fingers and having any woman you want slink to heel. Now, you might be quite happy with the sort of females who change their bed partner as casually as they change their nail varnish, but just take it from me—we're not all the same. Some of us employ a little discernment now and again, and some of us actually say no and mean it.'

'Really.' Black ice was making the airwaves freeze.

'Yes, really.' She continued to glare at him even as an image of the dole queue loomed strong. 'You are the last man, the very last man, I would offer a challenge to.' I've more sense for one thing, she thought wretchedly. You only have to touch me and I'm all gooey confusion. More fool me!

Now—in contrast to his cold, taut voice—the silence had begun to sizzle, and it took more effort than Cory would have believed possible to wrench her gaze from his and stare out of the window with as much cool as she could muster as she aimed for calm.

He might be the most spectacularly sexy man she had ever met—added to which she was head over heels in love with the rat—but that did not mean she was going to let him walk all over her, she told herself with a firmness she was proud of. And she didn't want to hear any other revelations about his past life either. She hadn't liked what his confidences had done to her. She'd wanted to fall into his arms, smother his face with kisses, convince him that there were still some good women left on the earth. But Max Hunter wasn't interested in *good* women, and the last thing he needed was a female who wanted to comfort and cherish him. Wear him out in bed maybe, but definitely not comfort and cherish him, Cory thought bitterly.

Neither of them spoke another word until they reached Narita airport, but Cory used the miles to claw back her aplomb and sense of proportion and give herself a good talking-to in the process.

It wasn't really Max's fault she had fallen for him, she told herself with brutal honesty. In fact he had warned her off in the first five minutes of seeing her. No, the fault was all hers. She had no one to blame but herself for this mess. And she shouldn't wage a war of words with him either—she knew there could only be one conclusion if she did. He was a ruthless opponent.

When the taxi drew into the airport confines she glanced at him from under her eyelashes. They couldn't work together after this—the journey home was going to be a nightmare as it was. Would he ask her for her resignation now or later? she thought miserably. Either way she had blown a fantastic job, but worse—a million times worse than that—she would never see him again.

'I'm not going to eat you for speaking your mind, Cory.' It was dry and mocking, and told her that her covert scrutiny had been noticed.

'And like I told you when you first came to work for me, I don't like boring women, and—whatever else—you're sure not that. I'm a big boy; I can take it on the chin.'

She met the tawny gaze warily. The last few weeks had taught her that Max was at his most dangerous when appearing calm and reasonable. That was the moment he usually went straight for the jugular, as many a savaged business colleague would testify to. 'I shouldn't have said all that I did,' she admitted after a long pause when he surveyed her through lazily narrowed eyes.

'Why? Because you think you were wrong?' he asked smoothly, his dark face giving nothing away.

'No, I do not think I was wrong!' It was very sharp and very swift. Eating humble pie was one thing but a whole meal quite another.

'Then I can only suppose you are following the adage of the boss is always right, and I've already told you what I think about that,' he said coolly. 'Don't be duplicitous, Cory. It doesn't suit you.'

'Duplicitous!' It was a splutter, and she had just opened her mouth to argue some more when he completely took the wind out of her sails by leaning across and depositing a swift kiss on her mouth a second before the taxi drew to a stand-still.

'Out you get,' he said with silky satisfaction at her red face. 'And I want to dictate a couple of reports while we're waiting for the flight, okay? There are a number of things I need down on paper while they're fresh in my mind.'

He was back in boss mode and Cory had the wisdom to know when she couldn't win, but as she walked into the airport building, Max's hand on her elbow and his big body towering at her side, she found herself wondering how he could manage to sweep their previous conversation aside so completely and set things back on course with such consummate ease.

But she shouldn't wonder, should she? she told herself in the next moment, the warning voice in her mind distinctly acidic. If there was one thing Max Hunter knew how to handle it was women—be they business colleagues, maiden aunts, girlfriends or secretaries! She didn't know where she stood with him from one moment to the next and she had the feeling that was the way he liked it.

He was a control freak. She played with the thought, turning it over in her mind, and she knew she was right. He let people get just so close and then no more; the door was slammed shut and the drawbridge hauled up. She wasn't quite sure if she had got the analogy right but she knew what she meant anyway, she told herself miserably. It could be summed up in one sentence. Max Hunter was bad news.

CHAPTER SIX

THE weeks following the Japan trip were frantic and passed in something of a blur, although a couple of things stood out from the hectic pace. One was blonde and one was brunette.

The first time one of Max's girlfriends sauntered into the office Cory was quite unprepared, and the beautiful blonde—who was all emerald-green silk Dior and ice-cool perfection—made her feel frumpy, fat and fatuous in the five minutes or so before Max took Karin—a Swedish model, he informed her in an aside, and had she noticed the immaculate nail varnish?—out for lunch.

Cory had ignored the sarcastic reference to their altercation in the taxi with a regalness she had been proud of at the time, and when the lunch had stretched to three hours and Max still wasn't back in the office she had told herself she didn't care what he was doing. Determinedly. Over and over again.

The brunette was a week later and just as gorgeous, and this time Max hadn't come back to the office before she had left at five. She hadn't slept at all that night, even though she had told herself she was the most stupid woman in all the world and she had to pull herself together— and fast. This was going to happen over and over again and she had to learn to deal with it if she wanted to stay in the job.

But did she? This thought had remained at the back of her mind when the blonde and brunette had faded somewhat. And as the weeks went on and spring blazed into summer it hadn't gone away.

Gillian had been right when she'd said Max was a boss in a million, Cory told herself one Monday morning in July when she arrived at the office to find she was accompanying Max and two colleagues to lunch at a very swish restaurant in the West End—again. He might be a human dynamo but he treated his staff very well, and the perks to being his secretary were amazing.

The meal was one of several she had enjoyed that month at Max's expense, along with one or two days out visiting associates and business contacts, and the job itself was fast, thrilling and absorbing, but... She sighed, staring at the screen of her word processor as though it was going to provide an answer to her torment. She was tearing herself apart.

Not that Max had ever attempted another embrace since that time in Japan, just the opposite in fact. He had been utterly businesslike at all times, cool, amusing, considerate, generous—the perfect employer of Gillian's description in fact. She had seen him being ruthlessly cutting on occasion, aggressive when the circumstances warranted it, plain nasty once or twice—but never with her. There might be just a touch of satire now and again, but only enough to make her smile.

And all that should make her very happy, shouldn't it? So why couldn't she rid herself of the notion he was keeping her very firmly at arm's length, that she wasn't seeing the real Max Hunter at all now? And why, if it was true, should it bother her so much? She couldn't have continued working with him—feeling as she did—if he had followed up on their brief love-making, she knew that, so this was for the best. Absolutely. Without question.

And her state of mind hadn't been helped much by the weekend she had just endured, and endured was certainly the right word, she thought irritably, her mind winging back over the preceding forty-eight hours, which had been hellish. She had gone home primarily for her last dress fitting and that had been bad enough;

Carole was a meringue and frothy lace person
and that was fine—the clouds of sequinned chiffon and satin suited the giddy blonde—but the
fact that the bridesmaids were attired in the
same style—and in bright pink—was something
else. The colour clashed horribly with the red
tint to her hair and made her skin look like weak
custard, and the fussy, over-the-top dress was
more suited to a young child.

Even Cory's mother—who had been roped in
by Vivian's parents to help with the arrangements after Cory's desertion to pastures new—
had been unable to dredge up the required response as she had seen her daughter emerge
from the village dressmaker's front room, and
had stared at her with a look of helpless sympathy.

And Vivian… Cory found she was glaring
into space now, and quickly forced her face into
office mode. What on earth was the matter with
Vivian? He had quite literally followed her
round all weekend like a little puppy; she hadn't
been able to get rid of him. Goodness knew
what Carole and everyone else had thought, but
she had found it highly embarrassing, not to
mention acutely irritating.

Twice he had tried to get her alone and twice
she had wriggled out of it, mainly because she

didn't want to hear what he might say, she admitted with more than a touch of self-recrimination. If Vivian was regretting his engagement he had to sort it out with Carole, not her, and there was no way she was getting involved. No way.

She sighed deeply and then shook her head at her own meanderings. She couldn't think of all that now; she had a desk full of work to deal with and then lunch at Bloomsbury's with Max and two important business contacts. She needed to be bright, sharp and focused. Anything less around Max Hunter and you were in trouble.

The telephone rang when she was in the middle of a complicated and extremely confidential report, and she lifted the receiver to her ear without taking her eyes off the screen, her voice preoccupied as she said, 'Yes? Mr Hunter's secretary. How may I help you?'

'Cory?' It was Mavis in Reception and she sounded a little flustered. 'There's someone here to see you.'

'To see me?' Cory asked in astonishment. 'Personally, you mean?'

'That's what he said. A Vivian Batley-Thomas? He says he's an old friend and that he thought you might be expecting him to call in some time today?'

'What?' It had been too loud and Cory cast an anxious glance at Max's interconnecting door before she said more quietly, 'I don't believe this; I had no idea he was coming, Mavis. Look, I'm terribly busy this morning; I'm in the middle of urgent stuff that just won't wait. Could you explain for me, please? I'll hold on.'

'Right.' Mavis hesitated a moment before she added, 'But he was very insistent he see you right now, Cory.'

She could imagine, Cory thought grimly. Vivian had a way of expecting the world to revolve around him, and why she had never seen it when she'd lived at home she didn't know. Or perhaps she did.

A good forty seconds ticked by, and then Mavis's voice came again, saying, 'He says he's only in London for a few hours, Cory, and it can't wait. A matter of life and death.'

Life and death, her foot! Cory frowned ferociously at the receiver, and then, as Max's voice cut across the room with, 'What the hell is that face for?' her eyes shot up to see him standing indolently in the doorway, the amber gaze trained straight on her face. Oh, perfect; this was all she needed on top of everything else!

He moved far too quietly for such a big man, Cory thought crossly. She'd noticed that about him before.

'Well? I take it this face has something to do with that?'

He gestured at the receiver in her hand and belatedly Cory realised poor Mavis was still hanging on for her reply. 'I'll be down in a moment, Mavis.' She replaced the receiver very carefully—the urge to slam it down was strong and it would be a mistake.

'Problem?' Max asked silkily. 'Can I help?'

He wasn't going to go away. Why was it that he seemed to *feel* trouble? Cory asked herself irritably. And she suddenly had no doubt that Vivian was going to prove exactly that.

'Not really,' she prevaricated jerkily. 'Someone has called in to see me, that's all. I had no idea they were coming...'

'Someone?' he asked smoothly. 'Care to be more specific?'

'An old friend.' She could feel herself flushing and it made her furious with herself but there was nothing she could do about it.

'Hmm.' His eyes had narrowed, moving slowly over her anxious face, and then he took her aback as he moved swiftly to her side, drawing her up and holding her an arm's length away as his gaze locked with hers. 'It's him, this Vivian guy, isn't it?' he said coolly. 'I wondered how long it would take him.'

'Take him?' Suddenly, in the space of a few seconds, their whole relationship had shifted again and it had knocked her for six.

'To realise he's made a big mistake,' Max said evenly. 'And now he's sniffing about seeing how he can back-pedal, eh? How do you feel about that, Cory? Have you got the sense and the guts to tell this creep to go to hell? Or would you like me to do the honours?'

His hands had tightened on her arms as he had spoken but that was the only indication of any emotion—his face and his voice were perfectly controlled and steady.

'I haven't even said it *is* him downstairs,' Cory protested weakly, her face glowing hotly. He was close enough for the smell of him to enfold her, its touch intoxicating on her senses, and as usual he had discarded his suit jacket and his tie as he'd been working. It wasn't the moment to feel a surge of desire but she couldn't help it.

Why did he always have to prance around half naked? Cory asked herself with wild exaggeration. Her nerves were quivering, her stomach muscles bunching, and the effect of him on her—her vulnerability where this man was concerned—made her voice sharper as she added, 'And it's none of your business anyway.'

'Wrong.' Now his strong fingers were actually hurting. 'Dead wrong. You start playing games with this guy and he'll tie you up in knots, and you'll be no good to me then. I want my secretary one hundred per cent dedicated and I pay for the privilege, as you well know. You knew what the job entailed when you took it on, Cory.'

The arrogance of it! Cory glared at him, rage surfacing in an overwhelming flood. He thought he owned her lock, stock and barrel, did he? Like some feudal lord keeping the peasants on his estate! She had never met anyone so full of their own importance as this man. Well, he could stuff his wonderful job—

'Besides which, I don't want to see you get hurt,' he finished more quietly, relaxing suddenly—something Cory felt was a definite decision on his part—as he said, 'I'm sorry, have I bruised you?'

'What?' She was staring at him, mesmerised by the change of tone and the softness apparent in the ruthless gold eyes. If anyone could tie her up in knots it certainly wasn't Vivian Batley-Thomas. 'Oh, yes, a little.' She rubbed at her

arms, folding her hands across her chest and taking a step back from him. 'It's all right.'

'Cory, I've met a hundred Vivians in my
time,' Max said softly, his gaze stroking her
troubled face. 'At the bottom of him he is weak
and that is why he is drawn to your strength. If
you take him on now you will be carrying him
for the rest of your life, you know that, don't
you? He is not the one for you. Believe me.'

She knew *that*. If nothing else she knew that,
Cory thought with a surge of hysterical amuse-
ment which she checked instantly. All this was
going to drive her mad before she was finished.
And then she spoke out the previous thought as
she said, her voice as firm as she could make it.
'I know Vivian and I could never get together,
Max. It's not an option as far as I'm concerned.'

'But he doesn't see it that way.' It was a statement, not a question, and the golden gaze was
pinning her to the spot.

'Possibly not.' She wasn't going to be drawn
into discussing this; Max had a way of eliciting
far more information than people wanted to give
at the best of times—and this wasn't the best of
times, not with Vivian waiting in Reception.

'I bet he doesn't.' For a second the control
wasn't absolute and she could have sworn there
was a snarl in the male voice, but then he

smiled, and amber eyes glowing a dark molten gold, as he repeated, 'I bet he doesn't,' his voice holding nothing more than mild irony now.

'No, well...' Cory found herself staring at him uncertainly, and she didn't like that. You couldn't be irresolute around Max. 'I'll just send him on his way, then.'

'You do that, Cory,' he said pleasantly.

She didn't know what it was—she couldn't have put her finger on it if it had meant her life—but there was something in the even dark tones that brought her head up a fraction and stiffened her back as she said, 'Don't worry, Max. I'll still get that report done in time and be ready to leave at lunchtime.'

'Damn the report.'

This time she knew she wasn't imagining the snarl, but in the next instant he had turned, strolling lazily into his office and shutting the door behind him with a gentleness that insisted she must have been wrong. But she hadn't been. She knew she hadn't been.

Cory spent another few seconds gazing at the door before she shut her eyes for an instant, screwing up her face before opening her eyes wide. And there was still Vivian... This was going to be one of those days it would have been better to have stayed in bed.

When Cory strode out of the lift at Reception she was all set to send Vivian away with the proverbial flea in his ear, but on her first sight of him as he sat, head down and with a kind of desperate look about him, her resolve melted.

'Cory!' He leapt up as soon as he saw her, his handsome face lighting up in a manner that would have once thrilled her. 'I had to come, you know that, don't you? I had to see you.'

'Hello, Vivian.' Cory was acutely conscious of Mavis's interested eyes, and now she drew him over to a small sofa sandwiched in between a prolific potted fern and a miniature palm tree. 'Is anything wrong?' she asked brightly, forcing a lightness to her tone.

'Is anything wrong...?' He gazed at her, his brown eyes velvet-soft and deep with liquid appeal. 'Cory, you have to forgive me. Please. I've been such a fool, such a stupid, mindless fool.'

This was going to be even worse than she had feared. 'Forgive you?' Cory smiled what she hoped was a brisk smile before saying, 'What on earth have I got to forgive you for, Vivian?'

'Oh, Cory.' It was almost a whine and everything in her rebelled at the sound. He was like a boy, she thought wonderingly, a selfish, spoilt brat of a boy, who had grabbed at what he thought was the best gift on offer and been presented with an empty box. But Carole wasn't an empty box, she was a live, warm human being, and after losing her parents when she was just a young child and growing up with a maiden aunt who had had little time for her she needed love and pampering and masses of attention. Which Vivian was obviously finding hard to give. But that was their problem, and they had to work it out together. She couldn't help him this time.

'I don't understand.' She looked at him steadily. 'What have I got to forgive you for, Vivian?'

'For leaving you, for hurting you,' he said softly. 'What we had was so good, Cory. I was stupid not to realise it at the time.'

'What we had was friendship, Vivian, and we still have it.' Cory looked him straight in the eyes and her voice was very clear. 'I shall always count you and Carole as two of my dearest friends.' It wasn't quite true but she felt the circumstances justified a little embellishment.

'You don't mean that.' His face had reddened and now there was a sharper note to his voice. 'You love me, you always have. You know we were meant to be together. This thing with Carole... It's just made me realise how much I love you, that's all. And it's not too late, Cory, don't you see? I want things back as they were.'

She'd rather die.

'I'll tell Carole. I'll tell her that I've seen you and we've realised we want to be together, that the wedding is off and—'

'*Vivian.*' She didn't shout but something in her voice stopped him in his tracks. 'Please don't go on. You made your decision and I think it's the right one. We would never have been happy together, not in a romantic sense. We're friends, that's all. It's the wedding and all the arrangements that's making you feel like this; lots of people experience wedding nerves—'

'Don't patronise me, Cory.' His face had gone pale and there was a tightness to his mouth that reminded her of the tantrums he had indulged in as a boy when he couldn't get his own way. 'I know why you ran away to London; it wasn't because you really wanted to leave, was it? You just couldn't bear seeing me and Carole together. I saw your face that night we got engaged. You want me, Cory.'

'I always think it's a mistake to assume you know what someone wants.'

Cory didn't know whether to be relieved or horrified when Max appeared round the side of the potted fern. He was his usual cool, urbane self, dark eyebrows slightly raised and a polite, courteous expression on his handsome face that she didn't trust for a moment.

'I apologise for the interruption,' he continued smoothly, 'but I really do need you upstairs, Cory, if you've finished here?'

'Max...' She stared at him in amazement before recovering almost immediately and saying, 'Max, this is Vivian, an old friend of mine. Vivian, this is my boss, Max Hunter.' She found herself waving her hands in an exaggerated gesture of introduction and stopped abruptly.

It was a valiant attempt but neither man was having it. Vivian looked at Max, taking in the wildly expensive designer suit, the perfect grooming, the handsome face, and his eyes narrowed. Max was making no attempt to hide his contempt of the other man—every little bit of body language was screaming out exactly what he thought of Vivian Batley-Thomas and a worm under a stone would have pre-eminence.

'So that's it.' Vivian's voice was a low hiss. 'I see it all now. How could you, Cory? How could you?'

'Is this some kind of code you indulge in in the country?' Max asked with suspicious calm. 'Shouldn't we be saying, ''how do you do?'' or something equally facetious?'

'How long has it been going on?' Vivian asked Cory, his face as white as a sheet now. 'And don't lie to me, Cory.'

'If you are an old friend of Cory's then you would know she never lies,' Max said icily, moving a step closer as he homed in on Vivian in much the same way a hunter sighted its prey. 'In fact she is painfully honest at times,' he added with a touch of dark humour.

'Now look, you, I don't know who you think you are—'

It was a mistake, and one which Vivian tumbled to immediately, as Max said, his face grim now and his eyes chips of hard amber, 'I know exactly who I am, Vivian.' He gave the other man's name a connotation that was plain insulting. 'I am Cory's employer and the owner of this building, so if you have finished your business with my secretary I suggest you get the hell out of here.'

'And if I haven't?' Vivian asked sulkily with a glance at Cory.

This was getting out of hand. Way, way out of hand. Cory found herself beginning to wring her hands and she stopped herself at once, forcing her voice into its normal pitch as she intervened quickly. 'Vivian, this is a working day, surely you understand that? You shouldn't have come here without letting me know first.'

'I had to. Cory, you know how I feel. I *had* to.'

'Wrong.' In contrast to Vivian's mumble, Max's voice was rapier-sharp. 'You chose to. And I want you out of here now.'

This was the worst scenario she could have imagined. How on earth was she going to act as chief bridesmaid and the supportive friend and neighbour now? Cory thought savagely. She could have handled Vivian if Max had left them alone; she knew she could. She hadn't needed him barging in with all the finesse of a steamroller.

'I'm in London overnight.' Vivian was speaking directly to Cory and his voice was desperate. 'Can I see you later?'

At that moment she would have promised anything to get Vivian out of the building and to bring an end to the farce, so she nodded her head abruptly. 'Phone me later at the flat. You've got the number, haven't you? We'll talk some more then, Vivian.'

'I'm asking you nicely one more time before I throw you out.' Max's voice was liquid ice and he had kept his eyes trained on Vivian.

'I'm going.' Vivian cast one more imploring glance in Cory's direction and then he turned, walking swiftly out of the building without another word, his head bowed and his shoulders sagging.

There was a second of utter silence and then Max said, his voice mockingly cruel, 'And that's the man you were eating your heart out for? I'm disappointed in you, Cory. You could do better.'

She didn't need this! A second before she had been feeling shattered by the encounter, and now she felt the adrenalin pour in like fire and its heat enabled her to draw herself up, her eyes flashing as she said, 'He might not be perfect but at least he isn't afraid of commitment and love.'

'Granted.' It was lethal. 'But it would help enormously if he could make up his mind exactly where that commitment and love should be, don't you think?' Max drawled cuttingly. 'I trust someone has explained the concept of polygamy is illegal in this country?'

Cory flushed hotly. He was hateful! 'Vivian's confused.'

'You're telling me,' Max agreed bitingly. 'Now, if you've quite finished billing and cooing with love's young dream, perhaps you would come and do a little work? Incidentally…' he paused, fixing her with a cold stare '…does his fiancée know he's panting on the leash and that you're providing a warm and comforting shoulder?'

He was insinuating that she had encouraged Vivian to chase after her? Cory's stare was equally cold as she said, her voice extremely tart, 'I really don't know, Max. Would you like me to give you Carole's number so you can enquire yourself?'

Eyes as cool as a deep sea-green lake locked with clear amber, and Cory saw him take a long, hard pull of air before he said, his voice scathing, 'I think you've done enough damage already, don't you? The poor girl is probably going through hell as it is.'

She was trembling deep inside and if they had been anywhere else but in Reception—anywhere—no power on earth would have stopped her slapping that arrogant, cold face. But executive secretaries didn't indulge in hysterics, she told herself grimly, however much they were provoked. 'That was cheap and uncalled for, and I wouldn't even justify it with an answer,' she said proudly, glaring at him one more time before brushing past him and walking towards the lift.

He joined her a moment later and as the lift doors opened allowed her to precede him into the carpeted confines. She had expected some retaliation but they stood in grim silence until the doors opened again on the hushed top floor, and then his voice was icy as he said, 'I want to see that report as soon as it is ready,' before stalking into his office. This time there was a definite bang and, ridiculous though it was, Cory found the brief lack of control on Max's part comforting. It showed she had managed to prick that rhinoceros hide just the slightest bit, if nothing else.

Cory worked hard the rest of the morning and she concentrated totally on the tasks in hand without allowing her mind to wander for even one moment. She would examine the events of the morning later—once she was home—but for now she didn't intend to give Max the opportunity to criticise her professionalism whatever else.

Max's lunch guests arrived at just after twelve and by twenty past they had all left the building for Bloomsbury's in Max's chauffeur-driven Rolls with Cory acting the cool, efficient secretary.

Bloomsbury's was a restaurant of some standing—all crystal chandeliers, damask linen tablecloths, elegantly smooth waiters and subdued conversation, but Cory had visited several times in the months she had been working for Max and was past being overawed. She acted the perfect hostess for Max and he was—as ever—the gracious host, but underneath the small talk and sophisticated banter she could feel the tension between them like the effect of a lightning storm on a migraine sufferer and it was draining.

By the time they were all back in the Rolls at just after three she found she was absolutely exhausted, although no one would have guessed from her bright face and easy conversation.

They dropped Max's business associates off first, and immediately the door of the Rolls closed behind them Cory felt the atmosphere inside the car tighten and electrify. She risked a sidelong glance at Max from under her eyelashes, but the dark profile was as inscrutable as always. How could one man be so *together*? she asked herself with understandable resentment. It just wasn't fair. She couldn't ever imagine him losing control or letting his guard down; he was one of the most unemotional men on the planet.

She settled back against the soft leather—they were still some miles from the office and she had to relax or explode—and for the first time since the encounter with Vivian allowed her mind to wander out of the tight confines she had kept it in the last few hours.

Her first thought, which had been hovering uneasily, was that Vivian had lied to her. He had supposedly called at the offices because he was just in London for a few hours—that was the message he'd relayed through the faithful Mavis—but then once she had met him he had stated he was in London overnight. She wasn't looking forward to this evening… She wanted to shut her eyes and lay her head back but such a show of weakness was unthinkable with Max sitting beside her. What could she say to Vivian that she hadn't already said this morning? she asked herself wretchedly. Whatever way you looked at it the evening was going to be awful, absolutely awful. Vivian knew how she felt, deep down, but he'd fight it.

Her thoughts continued to ebb and flow, and mainly because of them and the physical exhaustion the nervous tension of the day had caused it was some fifteen minutes later that Cory realised they were not on the right road. In fact she wasn't sure where they were, she told herself with a little start as she jerked upright in the seat and peered out of the window in alarm.

Max was lying indolently in his seat, his eyes closed and his breathing measured, but she knew instinctively the calm, relaxed pose was just that—a pose—and now her voice was sharp when she said, 'Where are we, Max? I don't recognise this area.'

He shifted slightly before opening his eyes, and once the piercing gold gaze met her anxious green one she felt her stomach turn over. He was up to something. 'We're in...' He sat up straight and peered out of the window. 'Pelham Street,' he said helpfully. 'It's just off Thurloe Square.'

Keep calm, keep calm, don't rise to the bait, Cory warned herself silently. She had seen this ploy of Max's with other people too often not to recognise what he was doing. He was contriving to rile her, to manoeuvre her into losing her temper while he sat back in apparent sympathetic—if slightly bewildered—benevolence, and to give him his due he'd had some spectacular results from what she'd seen. He reduced his opponent to teeth-grinding frustration, and then—when they were least expecting it—went in for the kill. *But not today, and not with her.*

'This is not the way to the office,' Cory stated grimly.

'No, no, it's not,' Max agreed genially. 'It's miles away.'

She bit down hard on her inner lip before she could manage, 'Then where are we going, Max?' And then, to avert further hedging, she asked flatly, 'Where is our ultimate destination?'

'I need some papers which are at home.' It was a cool statement and his face was deadpan. 'So it seemed opportune to call in.'

At home. Right, she could handle this. All she needed to do was stay in the car while he got the papers, that was all. Simple. She nodded abruptly, and then, when he shrugged off his jacket and indicated his tie with a 'Do you mind?' as he pulled it loose, she shook her head before turning to look out of the window.

Max's house was on the outskirts of Harlow, Cory had known that, but nothing had prepared her for the size of the grounds or the enormous mansion that came into sight once the chauffeur had opened the big security gates set in a stone-built, nine-foot-high wall and driven them up the winding pebble-covered drive.

'Cup of coffee?' The voice at her side was silky-smooth.

'What?' She drew her eyes away from the huge sprawling L-shaped residence that seemed to go on for ever, and then said hastily, 'Oh, no, thank you; I'll just wait here until you've got what you need.'

'I wouldn't hear of it,' he said easily. 'It will probably take a few minutes and my house-keeper would be mortified if I kept a guest wait-ing in my car that long without offering them refreshments.'

'I'm not a guest, I'm your secretary,' Cory pointed out.

'Mrs Brown wouldn't make that distinction.' There was a touch of steel beneath the smooth-ness now but Cory ignored it.

'I really would prefer to wait in the car,' she persisted politely.

'And I would prefer you to come in.'

She nerved herself to stare directly into the amber eyes and saw immediately he wasn't go-ing to give in. Over the last months she had learnt to read most of his expressions and she knew this one quite well—it was dig-your-heels-in time. 'If you insist....' She allowed her-self a resigned shrug and bored inclination of her head that suggested he was being tedious.

'I do, Cory.' His mouth curved into a sar-donic smile and then he had opened her door, alighting himself and then reaching out his hand to help her out of the car, his dark face cool and expressionless.

She extracted her hand from his the minute she was standing on the drive, but in the next instant he had taken her elbow, his fingers warm on her skin through the cotton material of the light summer jacket she was wearing and the scent of his body intoxicating.

'Come into my parlour said the spider to the fly.' It was a muttered aside as he shepherded her across the forecourt, up the semi-circular sweep of wide steps and then through the beautiful oak double front doors, and she ignored it. It wasn't difficult; she was having a job not to gasp out loud at what she was seeing.

The hall was majestic, there was no other word for it—from the beautifully polished wood floor to the high vaulted ceiling from which the bedrooms curved off balcony-style from the magnificent staircase—and just one of the exquisitely framed pictures on the brushed linen walls would have paid Cory's salary for six months.

'Come through to the drawing room.' Max led the way down the hall and into a room which was positively enormous and furnished in the sort of way most mere mortals just dreamed of. The carpet was cream-coloured and practically ankle-deep, the sofas and chairs a light honey and the scattering of fine antiques were tasteful and elegant and screamed unlimited wealth.

The huge French doors at the far end of the room, framed by long billowing cream silk curtains, led on to a beautifully laid out patio and beyond that there was a massive bowling-green-smooth lawn framed by mature trees with the glinting blue of a swimming pool in the far distance shimmering in the fierce July sun.

She shouldn't be surprised, Cory told herself silently as she gazed out at the sleeping garden. She had known he was a multimillionaire; he would hardly be living in a little three-bedroomed semi in the sticks, now, would he? But this... This really was beyond anything she had imagined. And quite overwhelmingly beautiful.

'Make yourself comfortable.' Max's voice was deep and soft behind her, and as she turned, a polite compliment hovering on her lips, she found herself just staring into his eyes instead. He was magnificent. Her mind said it all by itself as she looked into the dark, handsome face. And perfectly suited to these surroundings. He was as far from her orbit as the man in the moon. 'Would you like that coffee? Or maybe something long and cool?' he asked evenly.

'I...I'm fine.' Oh, don't stutter, she warned herself irritably. At least *try* and act as though all this hasn't blown your mind. He was used to women who took all this opulence in their stride without turning a hair. 'I'll just wait here until you're ready to go if I can't help at all,' she said with office politeness.

'Ah…' Now there was a dark note and she sensed it immediately. 'Well, that might be some time.'

She dared not voice her suspicions and instead said brightly, 'No problem, you're the boss.'

'Yes, I am, aren't I?' he agreed musingly.

It wasn't reassuring, but she was determined he wasn't going to intimidate her. She stared at him, keeping her face bland.

'The thing is, Cory, I've decided not to go back to the office today,' Max said smoothly. 'It's really doesn't fit in with my plans.'

She continued to stare at him, her green eyes showing more of their violet tinge as she struggled to keep the panic from showing, and then she kept her voice very steady as she said, 'Okay, if that's what you want. Shall I call a taxi or will the Rolls take me back?'

'The Rolls has gone.'

'So it's the taxi, then,' she stated briskly.

'Not…quite.' And then he had the audacity to smile as he added, 'There are five guest bedrooms to choose from.'

Cory's heart took a flying leap against her chestbone and then subsided into fluttering alarm. 'I'm going back to the office, Max.'

'No, you are not, Cory,' he countermanded in the same tone, his voice silky. 'You are staying here until tomorrow morning.'

'Are you mad?' she asked unevenly. He must be!

'I might be.' He surveyed her through half-closed gold eyes. 'It's been suggested before, I must admit. But of the two of us you are the craziest. That guy is a liability, Cory. I'm not going to let you get involved with him again. You need protecting from yourself.'

'You're not...?' The magnificent mansion faded away, his wealth and power disappearing with it, and now Cory forgot he was her boss, that her extremely generous salary and the numerous perks that went with it were under his control, and she fairly spat out her rage as she snapped, 'Who the hell do you think you are, Max Hunter? How *dare* you try and tell me what to do? I'm leaving here right now and you know what you can do with your job too. Employing me as your secretary did not mean you had the right to my soul as well.'

'Now as it happens it's not your soul I had in mind.'

He had jerked her into his arms before she realised what was happening, and as she began to struggle he subdued her as easily as if she were a child, guttural sounds of irritation in his throat as he bent his head to capture her evasive lips.

His mouth was hard and sensuous and it made her heart pound even more wildly, a trickle of warm desire flowing through her blood in spite of her very real fury. His tongue searched for hers, the thrust of its erotic insistency insidious against her rage as it caused excitement to flow where anger had been a moment before.

'Cory.' He gasped her name as his hands slid down her slender shape. 'Sweet Cory. Sweet, angry, elusive Cory.'

She was unable to offer more resistance as his touch became delicate and wonderfully persuasive, the desire that had him in its grip as fierce in her. He had moved her further into his hard frame, his hands on her hips as his hot arousal spoke of his own need, and as the kiss continued in all its intoxicating wonder she felt her limbs become fluid until it was only his arms that were holding her upright.

'Now tell me you want to meet him tonight,' he whispered against her ear some long minutes later when his mouth left hers. 'Tell me he can make you feel like this. Tell me you need him.'

His whisper jerked Cory out of the world of colour and light and sensation his lovemaking had taken her into and into the harsh reality of the present like nothing else could have done.

She pulled free, her legs trembling and her cheeks burning, but her eyes were sparking as she hissed, 'At least Vivian has never forced himself on a woman. He always conducts himself like a gentleman.'

'Yes?' His mouth had tightened. 'That doesn't surprise me. He's the type who would be content to be led about by a ring through his nose all his life,' he said, darkly fierce.

'Oh, so you're saying it's macho to use brute force?' Cory spat furiously, aware she was using anger to cover up her burning humiliation and shame. How could she have submitted so completely? she asked herself desperately. How could she? After everything she had told herself over the last months...

'Of course I'm not saying that,' he bit back tautly. 'I have nothing but contempt for anyone—man or woman—who thinks brute force can get them what they want.'

'Oh, come on!' She was fighting herself now, and the terrifying control he had over her, but he didn't know that. 'You don't expect me to believe that, do you? Actions speak louder than words after all.'

'I don't care what you believe, Cory,' he said with sudden and sinister quiet, 'but it's the truth. I got this—' he indicated the scar at the side of his throat which his open-necked shirt revealed more clearly and which she had thought about many times since she had first noticed it '—because someone thought they could force me to agree to what they wanted by employing such methods. They didn't,' he added darkly. 'I'm not an advocate of physical violence.'

She stared at him, too taken aback by the sudden revelation to be tactful as she said, her voice shaky, 'Who was it?'

'A lady friend.' He smiled but it was a mere twisting of the firm mouth, and chilling. 'She hadn't told me one little fact about our relationship when it was developing—namely that she had a husband—and when I found out I dumped her. She objected.' He lifted wry eyebrows.

'And she did that?' Cory asked in horror. His experiences with the female of the species seemed to bear more similarity to walking through a minefield than anything else.

'Yes, she did.' His voice was cold. 'But first she tried the old feminine tactic of threatening to kill herself if I didn't continue with our affair, and when that didn't work she flew into a rage and started throwing anything to hand. A Victorian hand mirror can do considerable damage, as I discovered to my cost,' he finished smoothly. 'The consultant told me that just the merest fraction one way and I would have bled to death within minutes. As it was it meant a damn inconvenient stay in hospital but that was all, and at least it taught me to be more careful in the future.'

'That's…that's awful.'

Cory was deeply shocked and it showed, and now Max shook his head slowly, his eyes cynical as he said, 'Carmen was no better and no worse than the rest of her sex, just a little more fiery than most, perhaps due to her Spanish blood.'

'You think *any* woman would be capable of such deceit?' Cory asked hotly. 'Not to mention physical violence? You can't believe that.'

'Yes, I do.' It was unequivocal. 'The human race has two great passions—greed and desire—and when either one is thwarted there can be trouble, but both together—that's when the fur flies.'

For a moment the enormity of the situation—which seemed to have blown up out of nowhere—made Cory speechless, but only for a moment. And then she straightened proudly, her eyes very green and very direct as she stared him full in the face. 'Then all I can say is that I am sorry for you, Max,' she said quietly. 'More sorry than I can say.' She saw the shock of her reply register in the hard male face but she didn't pause as she continued. 'You might be rich and powerful and you might have your world at your fingertips, but in reality you have nothing. You haven't got a clue what makes nice normal people tick, have you? And they're out there, believe it or not.'

'There is no such thing as a nice normal person, Cory,' he said tightly after a moment's deafening silence. 'We all have our dark side just waiting to rear its ugly head; some people just hide it better than others, that's all. I preferred the honesty of Carmen's attack to all her efforts at sweet persuasion.'

'She was one sick woman, Max.' Cory's chin raised itself another notch. 'And perhaps if you associate with such shallow, conniving people you got exactly what you deserved. Water always finds it own level—I'd have thought you knew that.'

'How refreshing…homespun wisdom,' he drawled nastily. But she had seen the look in his eyes and the sudden paling of his skin under its tan, and she knew her words had hit their target.

'No, just basic common sense,' she shot back quickly, hoping the trembling in her stomach wasn't communicating itself to her voice. She had spoken the truth when she had said she felt sorry for him, but that pity added to her love made her want to smother him in kisses, to give herself wholeheartedly without any reserve, and she knew that would be fatal. He wouldn't understand such a gesture; to Max it would be purely a physical expression of desire. But still her heart bled for him—for the lost little boy who had grown up with all the advantages in the world except the one that counted most—a mother's unconditional love that could have mellowed and softened even the worst of life's experiences.

'Then apply a little of that common sense to your situation.'

She had forgotten, just for a moment, that she was dealing with a razor-sharp intellect and ruthlessly focused mind, but now, as he brought the conversation back to her proposed meeting with Vivian, she saw that Max was still controlling the shots.

Cory stiffened, biting back the hot retort that had sprung to her lips and forcing herself to take a deep breath and count up to ten before she said, 'I have no intention of getting involved with Vivian, if that's what you're implying. Not that it's any of your business.'

'A bit of soft soap and he'll have you eating out of his hand in minutes,' he mocked silkily. 'He's the puppy-dog type.'

If she hadn't loved him so much she would have hated him. 'I'm sorry your opinion of me is so poor,' she said tensely, 'but as it's *my* life and *my* decision I would like to go now.'

He shrugged. 'No can do, I'm afraid. Sorry.'

'I shall ask your housekeeper to phone for a taxi,' Cory warned tightly, 'and I shall tell her why if necessary. You have no right to try and keep me here against my will. It's…it's barbaric! Not to mention illegal,' she added as an afterthought.

'You know, I'd quite forgotten Mrs Brown was visiting her sister overnight when I invited you here,' Max lied with careless ease. 'Silly of me. So it's just you and me, Cory.'

'You *planned* this?' She remembered he had been on the phone to his housekeeper when she had taken him a cup of coffee just after their morning altercation, and he had pointedly stopped talking until she had left the room. 'You did, you planned it,' she accused tautly.

'Of course.' The narrowed gold glare eyed her unrepentantly. 'You need protecting from yourself and there was no one else around.'

It was too much! The last straw! The final outrage!

'From myself?' The manipulating, devious, lying *swine*. 'You lure me here under false pretences, intending to keep me a virtual prisoner and try to get me to sleep with you, and you talk about *protection*?' Cory screeched angrily. 'You're unbelievable.'

'Sleep with you?' Max ignored the rest of her accusation with magnificent disregard. 'Cory, even among the shallow, conniving women I know it is customary to wait to be asked,' he said mildly. 'But of course I'm game if you are.'

'I'm not game!' she raged furiously, livid he had made her out to be some sex-crazy bimbo. 'I never will be. Not with you, Max Hunter, so you can forget it.'

'Pity.' He eyed her enigmatically. 'You tasted rather good.'

'I *insist* you let me leave,' she demanded autocratically.

'Don't be boring, Cory.' As he moved towards her again she tensed, but he merely took her arm, ushering her across the room as he said, 'Come and see your sleeping quarters and then change into a bikini. The pool is freshly cleaned and just waiting for us. And before you try, Mrs Brown unplugged and removed all the extension phones before she left and the master is in my study, the door of which is locked.' And he had the audacity to smile complacently.

'I wonder who could have possibly asked her to do that?' Cory snapped caustically. As if she didn't know!

'And there's a special code for the outside gate and the wall is unscalable, unless you've done mountaineering?' he asked mildly.

'You're unbelievable!'

'Thank you. It's nice of you to mention that again, especially as you haven't experienced all my attributes yet,' he murmured smoothly. 'Or not to their fullest potential, anyway, but of course we can rectify that any time you like. Now, I'm sure there will be swimwear to fit you in your quarters along with anything else you might need, so why don't you relax and enjoy the evening now you are here? A couple of hours relaxing by the pool followed by a good bottle of wine and a leisurely meal isn't *too* much of an ordeal, is it? You might even find you like me a little by the end of the night,' he added sardonically. 'Miracles do occasionally happen.'

If he only knew! It was that thought that silenced anything further Cory might have said, but as she allowed Max to lead her out of the drawing room and towards the stairs she was praying like she had never prayed before.

CHAPTER SEVEN

WHEN Max left her with a casual, 'See you in ten minutes downstairs,' after opening the door of what appeared to be a sumptuous guest suite, Cory stood for some moments just inside the room without moving. Oh, wow! Wow, wow, and treble wow, she thought weakly.

She was standing in an area which was obviously a small sitting room, and the normal furnishings were complemented by an ultra-modern flat-screened television, a hi-fi system complete with an extensive range of CDs, and what looked like a fridge and small bar. The decor was a deep dark rose and dull gold, like a dying sunset, and she could see the same colours reflected in the bedroom beyond, which was approached through a gracious arch at the far end of the sitting room. The *en suite* was in gold and cream marble and complete with Jacuzzi, and when she gingerly opened the walk-in wardrobe she saw enough outfits—all with designer labels—to kit out ten female guests. Guests? Lovers, she thought caustically.

But it wasn't the flagrant display of unlimited wealth that was making her heart thud, it was Max himself. She didn't understand this—the way he was acting—and neither could she quite take in that the world she had inhabited this morning had changed quite so dramatically in just a few short, action-packed hours.

This morning he had been merely her boss—Max Hunter, business tycoon and playboy extraordinaire—and in that capacity she could cope with her feelings regarding him, almost. But now... Now she wasn't quite sure what he was or how he saw her, and it bothered her more than she would have thought possible. Because she was weak where he was concerned—that one passionate embrace in the drawing room had confirmed it all too succinctly, and being alone with him like this was a recipe for disaster. And she didn't need it.

Why had Vivian appearing on the scene that morning got under his skin quite so fiercely? she asked herself now as she plumped down on the huge bed with a little sigh. He wasn't particularly interested in her—he'd made that quite plain over the last weeks since their brief lapse from boss/secretary mode in Japan. And even *that* had only been because he had thought she was available, she reminded herself miserably.

Once she had spelt out how she felt he had left her well and truly alone. Her only redeeming feature, as far as he had been concerned, was that she wasn't boring, and he'd even accused her of that this afternoon!

What was she going to do? She sat for some sixty seconds more in the warm, faintly perfumed room, before jumping up from the bed and walking over to the wardrobe again. Well, if she wasn't going to sulk in this guest suite till morning there was only one other alternative, she decided bravely. She would go down to the pool as Max had suggested and act as cool and contained as any ice-queen.

Disdainful. As she surveyed the beautiful clothes she nodded at the word. That was what she would be. He had an ego as big as a barn door and she was blowed if she was going to be another notch on his belt. Two could play at the love-'em-and-leave-'em game!

She fetched out and discarded two or three minuscule scraps of no doubt wildly expensive material that were masquerading as bikinis, before her eyes alighted on a slightly more sedate swimming costume. The delicately shaded material flowed from dove-grey through to deep violet, and if it fitted she would feel somewhat less exposed in a one-piece, Cory decided as she quickly began to undress.

She felt a little less sure about the swimwear once she was staring at herself in the mirror some moments later, however. The costume was sensational but undoubtedly provocative. The cut of the legs went to waist level and the deep plunging neckline met it, with just a precarious ribbon of material holding the whole thing together. It made her somewhat small but full bust look great, she thought with a touch of pleasure despite the circumstances, and her legs went on for ever, but the thought of displaying her wares in front of Max was daunting to say the least.

She remained in irresolute silent contemplation for some seconds more, before a sense of 'in for a penny, in for a pound' bravura swept over her. The costume went hand in hand with a transparent silky shirt top of the same material—a beautiful thing on its own—and if nothing else the outfit screamed panache. And if ever she'd needed panache it was now. When she thought of the women Max was used to...

When she swept downstairs some minutes later no one would have dreamt her stomach was doing cartwheels and she was scared to death.

Max was waiting in the hall and in the second she caught sight of him before he raised his head Cory received a lightning bolt straight through her body. Normally his dark good looks were more than devastating enough, but nearly naked he was dynamite. The broad, hard-muscled shoulders, big lean frame and powerful legs were relaxed in casual ease as he half lay sprawled in an easy chair at the foot of the stairs, and after her first glimpse of acres of hard, tanned, sinewy male flesh Cory kept her eyes on a point just above his head.

When her flip-flops reached the polished wood of the hall floor Cory nerved herself to meet Max's waiting narrowed gaze, and she saw his eyes were intent on her face as he rose to meet her, and he wasn't smiling. He was wearing just the briefest of swimming trunks.

'You look beautiful.' It was deep and low and made her shiver inside. 'Except...' He reached out and turned her round, loosening her hair from its pins and ignoring her protests. 'Now that's better.' There was a great deal of manly satisfaction in his tone as her rich, long dark brown hair tumbled about her shoulders. 'You should always wear your hair like that,' he added quietly as he turned her about to face him again. 'I've told you before.'

Cory shrugged in what she hoped was a sufficiently calm way to fool him into thinking she could have spoken if she'd wanted to, but in reality the closeness of that powerful male chest with its light dusting of black body hair had frozen her vocal cords and caused her legs to become liquid jelly.

'There's an ice bucket and champagne waiting for us by the pool,' Max said silkily as he took her arm and drew her towards the open drawing-room door. 'And strawberries of course. There is nothing nicer than champagne and strawberries on a lazy summer's afternoon, is there?'

She wouldn't know, Cory thought with a stab of pain, although she had no doubt this was a ploy Max had used with his women many times in the past. Although she wasn't one of his women, was she? She was his secretary. *That was all she was.* And she had better keep the fact at the forefront of her mind, she added caustically as they passed through the French doors and into bright sunlight, because she had the feeling Max wasn't going to.

They were halfway across the lawn when Max stopped, turning to enclose her lightly in his arms with his hands in the small of her back as he said, his tone reproving and faintly disappointed, 'How long are you going to keep the icy, silent approach up, Cory? I hadn't figured you for a poor loser.'

She knew exactly what he'd figured her as! The embrace in the drawing room and the champagne and strawberries spoke volumes! But it wasn't sulkiness that had kept her quiet, it was him, Max Hunter—although she would rather die than admit to the desire that was snaking through her limbs and making her fluid.

'Kidnapping is a criminal offence,' she said shakily as she stared up into his face. His great height made her feel as though she was tiny and delicate and utterly feminine and it wasn't an unpleasant sensation, neither was the feeling that she was enclosed in steel coated with the veneer of warm flesh.

'Then you can report me tomorrow,' he said silkily.

She could feel the hard thud-thud of his heart against her fingers where they were resting lightly against the broad chest, and smell the intoxicating fragrance of fresh male skin and expensive aftershave, and it was heady.

'But for now...' He eyed her coolly, his gaze stroking over the lovely flushed face framed by the glowing red-brown waves that shone myriad shades in the white sunlight. 'For now you accept this is *fait accompli* and lover-boy is going to go home to his faithful future spouse disappointed, okay?'

Lover-boy? She had so completely forgotten Vivian that it took a moment to understand what he was talking about, and then it was guilt at her utter detachment from Vivian and his troubles that made her voice tart as she said, wriggling a little now, 'What gives you the right to meddle in people's lives like this anyway?'

'Nothing and no one *gives* me anything, Cory,' he said smoothly. 'I take what I want. Isn't that the name of the game when all is said and done?' He raised mocking, quizzical eyebrows at her cross face.

'*Your* game maybe.' She frowned up at him, her eyes sparking, and then he cut through all her defences when he grinned, his face relaxing and his rare smile lighting up the darkness that was always hovering at the back of his eyes, as he dropped a light kiss on the tip of her nose before sweeping her up into his arms, saying, 'Come on, you stubborn wench; a good dunking in the pool will wash away that pout and cool you down.'

'Don't you dare! Max! Don't you dare throw me in!'

She was struggling in earnest now but it had about as much effect as a tiny fly caught in a massive spider's web.

'You can swim?'

They had reached the edge of the pool now and for a moment she thought about lying but it was too late—he had read the truth in her eyes. The next moment she found herself flying through the air into the silky cold depths, and she just had time to hold her nose before going under the water in a tangle of arms and legs.

When she surfaced Max was treading water at the side of her, his mouth still curved in that grin that made him look like an overgrown boy, and it was that which made her voice weak as she said, 'You pig! That was really mean, you pig.'

'Careful.' He held up a warning finger, his eyes glinting with laughter. 'You're very vulnerable in here.'

She was very vulnerable anywhere if he was around, Cory thought as a surge of love made her wish from the bottom of her heart that things were different. But they weren't and they would never be.

'Can I at least put this on the side, please?' She tried to make her voice stern but it merely sounded breathless as she indicated the shirt top she was in the process of shrugging off.

'Of course.' His gaze was narrowed as he watched her swim with firm, strong strokes to the side of the pool and toss the sodden top onto the hot tiles, and his voice was approving when she swam back. 'You're an excellent swimmer; you swim like a man.'

'Is that supposed to be a compliment?' she asked mockingly. 'Women are able to do most things as well as—if not better than—men given half the chance.' She grimaced at him cheekily and he smiled back.

'Most of the women of my acquaintance are too worried about their hair and make-up to bother to learn to swim at all,' he said wryly. 'Pools are for posing by. Full stop.'

'I've told you before, Max, you mix with the wrong women.' It was too good an opportunity to miss, but Cory didn't wait for his reply, turning in one slender movement and cutting through the water with a powerful crawl to the deep end of the Olympic-size pool.

'Where did you learn to swim like that?' He had followed her but Cory had been pleased to see he hadn't been able to catch her up. 'I hadn't got you down as a woman athlete.'

'My father's a great swimmer, my mum too.' Cory raked back her hair from her face and grinned at him. 'The three of us did a course in scuba diving some years back, and once you've trained in a quarry in November in freezing cold water and taken your mask off ten metres under, and had what feels like a ton of ice hit you full in the face, anything else seems easy. My father and I continued with the advanced course but my mother had had enough by then.'

'Right.' He was surprised—she could tell by the expression deep in the gold eyes—but he was trying to hide it. It felt marvellously—*fabulously*—good to have taken him aback. 'Have you swum abroad?' he asked interestedly. 'Gone down in warm waters?'

'A few times, on package holidays—nothing elaborate,' Cory said evenly. 'Nevertheless the water was a good few degrees warmer and it was fascinating to swim down and see the different sea life to England. It's a whole different world down there.'

She launched off the wall of the pool as she finished speaking, glorying in the feel of the clean clear water on her warm skin, and this time Max was just behind her when she reached the shallows.

'A real-life water baby.' His eyes were warm and his voice more so, and Cory didn't like what it did to her heart. He was too attractive and a darn sight too charming, she warned herself firmly as a little warning bell clanged shrilly in her brain. In fact Max Hunter was too much of everything! 'You obviously get on well with your parents?' he asked now, his voice probing.

'They're great,' Cory affirmed shortly. She didn't want to discuss her parents with Max; in fact the less he knew about her private life the better. She knew every little bit of personal information would be stored in that computer-like brain and analysed to his own advantage, and who knew when or how he would use it?

He nodded slowly, the drops of water moving like diamonds in the sunlight over his tanned skin and making her muscles clench. 'It's a great gift, a loving upbringing,' he said quietly, and for once there was no cynicism or amusement in the dark voice. 'My father loved me but he had no time to show it, and when there might have been a chance of us getting to know each other—after I'd left university—the time ran out.'

And then, as though regretting the brief opening of the window into his mind, his expression changed and the window was slammed shut and his tone was merely teasing as he said, 'I'll race you if you think you're up to it? You being a mere woman, that is.'

'Ha! I could beat you with one hand tied behind my back,' Cory challenged immediately.

She didn't, but neither did Max outdo her, and for a good few lengths—as they swam up and down in the blazing sunshine—they were neck and neck, until Cory found herself tiring. Max, it seemed, could go on for ever, and for some ten minutes after she had climbed out of the water and was sitting on the side of the pool he continued to cut through the clear blue depths like a machine. An incredibly sexy, live, warm, breathing machine who had a body erotic dreams were made of, Cory told herself ruefully.

She was no longer the same person since she had met him. It was frightening but true. And she couldn't imagine a world in which she didn't see him, watch him, feel him about her. And that was even more frightening. What she'd felt for Vivian…it just didn't bear any resemblance to this fierce, consuming emotion that was eating her up from the inside. But it was destructive and very, very dangerous.

'Right, a glass of champagne, I think.' He hauled himself out beside her and then stood in one lithe movement, offering her his hand as she continued to sit on the side of the pool. She had put on the shirt top as she'd sat watching him, and now she pulled the edges together, hastily fastening two or three of the buttons before she took his hand and rose to her feet.

'It's useless, Cory.' He eyed her intently, his skin gleaming.

'What?' His voice had been deep and husky, and she was painfully aware of the powerful body just inches from hers.

'Trying to cover yourself up,' he said softly. 'You could clothe yourself in black from head to foot and I'd still see those long, slender legs and tiny waist and wonderful breasts.'

'Max, don't do this.' There was a note of panic in her voice, and now his expression hardened, his eyes taking on the brilliance of liquid gold as he stared into her defensive face.

'Why?' His look was heated and angry. 'I want you, you know that, damn it, and you want me whatever you're telling yourself to the contrary. It's been slowly killing me the last few weeks, working in the same office, seeing you sitting at that desk with your hair hidden from view in those ridiculous buns. The times I've wanted to rip your clothes off and take you then and there on that same desk and to hell with the consequences.'

'That's lust, plain and simple,' she shot back tightly.

'It might be plain but it's sure not simple.' He scowled angrily. 'I'm sick of cold showers umpteen times a night.'

Cory was still battling with the image he had conjured up in her mind regarding her plain little serviceable desk—she'd never be able to look at it in the same way again—but she struggled to keep her quivering from showing as she said, 'I don't do cheap affairs, Max. I thought I'd made that clear. And you've told me yourself you aren't into anything else, so why are we having this conversation?'

'I *told* you I believe in enjoying a member of the opposite sex—and them enjoying me—without the illusion of happy ever after,' Max grated. 'That's why.'

'That's what I mean.' She faced him squarely, her eyes shadowed as she tried to keep her lips from trembling. 'Cheap affairs.'

'Hell!' His eyes had skimmed over her face and now he pulled her into his damp body with a roughness that spoke of inner turmoil. 'You're so damn stubborn you should have been born a man!'

She wanted to fight him but she just didn't have the emotional strength, and as she relaxed against him with a tiny stifled sob she felt him stiffen. He continued to hold her for some moments without speaking, the hot sun beating down on them, and then he said, still without moving her from him and with her face buried in the male, scented warmth of his shoulder, 'Why aren't you tough and hard like all the others, for crying out loud? Why are you tearing me apart inside? I eat you, sleep you, breathe you, work you...'

It was an unexpected confession and Cory was too dazed and bemused by his words—and his nearness—to even attempt to answer. He was like a fierce black whirlwind, sweeping everything it came into contact with into its orbit, she told herself tiredly, too shattered to think clearly. But if she gave in to him, if she let herself be absorbed into the swirling, spinning tornado that was Max Hunter, she would be drained and consumed of everything that was the real her. And she couldn't let that happen. Because it *would* end.

Max's fingers had started to stroke her back, their touch mesmerising, and now she arched back from him but he continued to hold her fast as he said softly, 'I can't help it, Cory. I want you all the time, I'm aching for you, and the thought of that insensitive, undeserving so-and-so pawing you about…'

'Vivian?' She raised her head now, too astonished at what she saw as his hypocrisy to watch her words. 'How have you got the nerve to call *him* insensitive when you are the world's worst on that score?' she asked in vehement outrage, thinking of the sleepless nights and constant turmoil she had suffered since she had first set eyes on this man. 'Anyway, you don't even know Vivian,' she added angrily.

'I don't have to.'

It was said with supreme arrogance, and then, as Cory opened her mouth to argue some more, his mouth took hers, his lips sensuous and horribly persuasive as his tongue began to fuel the fire.

He kissed her until she was gasping for breath and aching, her body betraying her completely as her breasts became full and swollen against the hard, solid wall of his chest, her nipples thrusting against the thin silk of the swimming costume and transparent top.

'You see, you do want me.' His hand brushed one full breast and she moaned out loud before she could stop herself, and then, as the sound echoed in her ears, Cory jerked away from him, her face scarlet. He had to prove his point. All the time, he had to be right.

'I don't.' It was a whisper but he heard it and his firm mouth twisted at the blatant lie, his eyes narrowing mockingly.

'Sure you do.' He smiled, but it wasn't the open, sweet smile that had wrung her heart earlier. 'And you'll tell me that when you're ready. I can wait till then, Cory. I've never yet taken a woman who wasn't wholly and completely ready—mind and body—and I don't intend to start with you, however much I'm tempted.'

His body was providing ample truth of just how strong that temptation was and she shivered deep inside. She wanted to come back with some clever, witty retort, something to prove she was on a par with his other sophisticated, worldly women even if she didn't share their views on life and love, but she couldn't. If she had spoken at that moment she would have burst into tears. She loved him so much and this was all such a mess.

'Come on.' He took her elbow, his touch light and casual now, but as they walked over to the far corner of the area around the pool which was shaded by a massive willow tree she was vitally aware of every movement of that magnificent body.

There were loungers and small tables all round the pool at strategic points to catch some shade, but this tiny idyll was in a small semi-circle of flowering bushes that smelt wonderful, their fragrance reminiscent of magnolia flowers and hot exotic nights.

Two cushioned loungers had been placed at either side of a low rectangular table holding a large ice-bucket in which a bottle of champagne nestled, and alongside were two tall fluted glasses of delicate crystal and an enormous bowl of strawberries. Two smaller bowls, spoons and even a dish of cream, again nestling in ice, were close by. Everything was perfect. Too perfect.

He really did think of everything. Cory eyed the cosy little setting with uncharacteristic cynicism and the champagne with definite wariness, glad of the substantial lunch they had enjoyed earlier in the day at Bloomsbury's. A master of seduction, no doubt. But this time all his careful arrangements would come to nothing.

Max thought she merely fancied him and that was all—his earlier comments had made it clear he wasn't even sure if she liked him very much—and he also thought she had slept with Vivian and probably other boyfriends in the past. Therefore, by his reckoning, a brief dalliance with himself was quite on the cards. No one would get hurt and he had been very careful to lay out the ground rules.

But she would get hurt. Cory sat down gingerly on one of the loungers and watched him as he flung himself on the other one, one lean muscled arm reaching out for the champagne a moment later. If she had merely been attracted to him as he thought, Max Hunter would have been a hard act to follow, but loving him as she did... It would destroy her when he tired of her body and decided enough was enough; she just wasn't tough enough to cope with it.

She wanted to give herself to him body, soul and spirit—to become one with him in the biblical sense, to have children, build a family and home and he didn't even have any understanding of such a concept. And he'd laugh himself silly if it was suggested to him.

'Here.' She came out of the dark morass of her thoughts to find a glass of sparkling champagne under her nose, its effervescent exuberance mocking her misery. 'Eat, drink and be merry.'

'Because tomorrow we die?' She finished the old saying with a touch of whimsical amusement she was proud of in the circumstances.

He gave a sardonic smile that was so sexy it made her toes curl. 'Oh, no, Cory,' he said softy as he guided the glass to her lips with a firm hand. 'I wouldn't allow you to escape me like that. I want to teach you how to live.'

'I know how to live,' she objected quickly. 'I enjoy my life.'

'No, you don't, not yet, but you will,' he promised slowly. 'But for now...' The glass was again steered to her lips. 'Relax.'

It was wonderful champagne, Cory thought as she sipped at the fragrant, slightly strawberry-tasting liquid with very real pleasure. It knocked anything she had tasted before—which had masqueraded under the same name—into a cocked hat. But any sense of well-being it gave was short and transitory, as ephemeral as the morning dew on a summer's morning, and that was exactly how an affair with Max would be. As fleeting as a half-remembered dream.

The thought provoked her to say, as she placed the glass on the table and then turned to face the amber gaze directly, 'Correct me if I'm wrong, but it was you who said that an affair with your secretary would be nothing more than a nuisance at best and at worst downright dangerous, wasn't it?' she asked sweetly. She had never forgotten his words on that first day, or how angry they had made her feel.

He nodded slowly, his eyes smiling at her. 'You're the exception that proves the rule,' he said with audacious seriousness.

'And you really think that we could conduct an affair and still work together?' Cory asked quietly without an answering smile.

'Possibly.' He was watching her very closely. 'Yes, why not?'

'And when it ended?' she persisted quietly. 'What then?'

'We're two grown adults,' he answered calmly. 'If there was honesty between us from the beginning I don't see it being a problem. You are not the type to get all bitter and twisted.'

'Max, you don't have a clue what "type" I am,' Cory shot back tightly, stung beyond measure by his terminology.

'It was meant as a compliment.' He had immediately realised his mistake and now the charm was out in full force, Cory noticed irritably as he sat up straight and then leant across to take her hands in his. 'Truly, Cory, I think you're gorgeous,' he said huskily, releasing her hands to cradle her angry face in his hands. 'Utterly gorgeous and warm and sexy and wonderful.'

So this was how he was with his women, Cory told herself silently. It was a side to him she hadn't seen so far and it was absolutely lethal. And of course he knew it; he knew it only too well.

'And you were right, you know, when you said I got what I deserved with this.' He touched the side of his throat briefly. 'I've always gone for the packaging without bothering to unwrap the parcel; it was safer after the Laurel and Anne affair. That way no mistakes could be made.'

Oh, no, she didn't trust him like this. He could tie her up in knots with this little-boy-lost approach and she had the feeling he knew it. Her thoughts made her voice tart when she said, 'I'd consider the woman behind the hand that wielded that mirror something of a major hiccup in that thinking?'

He stared at her for a moment as she looked boldly back at him, and then he amazed her by throwing back his head and giving a bellow of a laugh. 'I walked into that one, didn't I?' he said with a rueful self-deprecation that made her love him more. 'Right, well, as I'm not going to seduce you by throwing myself on your feminine compassion, we might as well relax and enjoy ourselves, eh? A few strawberries, another swim, and then more champagne. No strings attached and no ulterior motives. How does that sound?'

'Okay.' It was tentative, and again the bellow echoed round the garden as she watched him in amazement.

'Cory, you're one on your own.' He had leant forward to take her mouth in a light kiss as he had spoken, and then he surprised her by stopping abruptly inches from her lips, his brow creasing in a slight frown as he continued to stare into the violet-splashed green eyes for long moments. 'One on your own,' he echoed softly.

'Max?' His expression disturbed her. 'What's the matter?'

'The matter?' He came back to her with visible effort, his face clearing as he noticed her worried face. 'What could be the matter?' he prevaricated easily. 'I've got the most beautiful woman in London at my side and the night is young.' But his eyes had hardened and his mouth had straightened—she had seen it—and now the charm was definitely forced. Something had happened.

She stared at him for a moment more but then he turned away to fill two bowls with strawberries, and when he turned back to her his face was clear and open, and she told herself she must have imagined the expression of what had appeared to be stunned comprehension.

They swam and dozed, and ate and drank, and then swam some more in the sleepy, sluggish air, until the heat of the day had been swallowed up in a mauve-tinged mellow dusk that filled the sultry garden with warm shadows and the scents of evening.

It was well past eight o'clock by the time they retraced their footsteps to the house, and in all that time Max had behaved with a circumspect correctness that Cory couldn't quite understand. But it was good, she told herself firmly as Max left her at the door of her suite after telling her to dress for dinner in an hour or so. It really was good. And this feeling of pique, even hurt, that had grown through the afternoon after their earlier conversation—that was just her stupidity of wanting her cake as well as eating it.

She ran herself a warm bath, and once she was lying in the foaming, bubbling water of the Jacuzzi she refused to let herself dwell on the feelings that were just pure self-indulgence on her part. She had told Max she didn't want to get involved and he had finally decided to accept it. End of story. If she was thinking of anyone it really ought to be poor Vivian, she told herself guiltily. He'd be ringing her bedsit all evening and wondering why she wasn't picking up the telephone. He'd think— Oh, she didn't care what he thought! And why was she thinking like this anyway? she asked herself.

She sprang out of the water and marched through to the bedroom, her face one big scowl. She was in a ridiculous position here, and Max had a lot to answer for, but the person who was really to blame was Vivian Batley-Thomas. How *dared* he slink down here and try to ascertain whether she was prepared to welcome him with open arms before he got up the nerve to give Carole the old heave-ho? Because that was what all this boiled down to, she told herself firmly. It wasn't a case of 'poor Vivian' at all! Poor Carole, more like.

She walked through to the sitting room and selected a CD of what she hoped was tranquil, soothing music, turning the volume up reasonably high as she went back into the bedroom to decide what to wear for the evening in front of her.

After choosing the least alluring dress she could find—not an easy task in the sexy contents of the wardrobe—Cory creamed her honey-toned skin and dried her hair, before standing stark naked in front of the long bedroom mirror as she scowled at the slender, dark-haired reflection in its misty depths.

Men! They were all selfish, egotistical, manipulating brutes at heart with just one thing on their minds. She looked at herself, her eyes moving critically over the long, well-shaped legs, the small waist and pert full breasts. Nothing special. She sighed, her heart aching, and shut her eyes for a few seconds as she thought about the other females—the incredibly beautiful other females—who were falling over themselves to be seen with Max. She had no chance of ever changing his mind about life and love, she knew that, so why had today hurt so much? Why couldn't she accept things?

'Cory?'

For a moment she really thought her deepest longing had conjured up an echo of that dark voice, and she sighed again at her weakness, thinking wryly, First sign of madness, along with talking to yourself!

And then she opened her eyes.

The reflection in the mirror had changed. Now Max was standing in the arch that led to the bedroom from the sitting room with his eyes glowing like the eyes of a big cat as he stared straight at her.

CHAPTER EIGHT

'I KNOCKED.'

As Cory whirled to the bed, grabbing the scanty dress and holding it against her, the only thing that moved was Max's mouth.

'Get out.' She spoke through clenched teeth, trying to ignore the fact that the dress barely covered half of what needed covering. 'There's a name for men like you,' she hissed furiously

'Misunderstood?' He had registered her outrage. 'I told you I knocked but with that damn music full blast you probably didn't hear me. What are you trying to do? Wake the dead?'

'Of course I didn't hear you!' She glared at him, her arms crossed against her breasts and the dress hanging down in front of her. 'And that still didn't give you the right to barge in here like this,' she spat hotly. 'Now will you please leave?'

'I didn't barge, Cory. I knocked—twice—and then I called as I opened the door.'

'Well, bully for you.' She had never been so embarrassed in her life and attack was the best defence. 'But for the third time of asking—

223

would you like to leave now?' she ground out
tightly.

'We both know what I would like to do.' It
was dark and there was no humour at all.

'I'm warning you, Max. You lay a finger on
me and—'

'You don't have to warn me, Cory,' he said
tautly. 'I know your opinion of me is low but
even I wouldn't stoop to what you're suggesting. Get some clothes on.' The last was said as
though she had purposely paraded in front of
him and it was thrown over his shoulder as he
turned away. It made Cory so mad she couldn't
contain herself and all her prudence was burnt
up in the fire of anger.

She pulled the silk cover off the bed in one
violent movement, sending the underclothes that
had lain next to the dress flying in the air, and
as she threw the dress to the floor she wrapped
the cover round her sarong-style before leaping
after Max like an enraged tigress. He was halfway across the sitting room when she bit out his
name and he turned without a word, his amber
eyes looking at her with what she was sure was
contempt.

'I've had enough! Of you, this—' she flung
out her arms wildly to embrace the beautiful
room '—the whole situation, including your

wonderful job!' She was so angry she was shaking.

'Do I take it you are offering your resignation?' Max asked with an unforgivable lack of emotion.

'I'm telling you I quit,' Cory shot back tightly. She couldn't take any more of this; she really couldn't. Seeing him every day had been bad enough, working with him, having to talk and laugh and act as though he meant nothing more to her than little Martin, the office junior, but now she knew how he felt... It was an impossible situation. Sooner or later she would give herself away and then her last defence would be gone. 'As of now.'

'You're under contract,' he reminded her coldly. 'You can't quit.'

'Then sue me.'

'You're being ridiculous,' he bit out, his voice sharp now.

'But *normal* people are ridiculous at times,' she shouted angrily, stamping her foot at his infuriating *togetherness*. 'We do crazy things, we make mistakes, we aren't perfect. We even love the wrong people sometimes.' She hadn't meant to add that bit.

'So you admit Vivian is the wrong person?' he grated tightly.

Vivian? She wasn't talking about *Vivian*, she thought desperately, if only he did but know it. 'Vivian is nothing to do with it,' she snapped furiously, 'not really. I'm saying that it's normal to lose control sometimes, to fail, to be *human*, for goodness' sake. But you, you're too darn scared to even dip your toe in the water of real honest-to-goodness emotion, aren't you? The original ice-man! All cool, macho love-'em-and-leave-'em and what the hell!'

She knew she was going too far—the blazing anger on his face would have told her that if nothing else had—but something had broken in the last few minutes and no power on earth could have stopped her now.

'You're just a coward at heart, Max Hunter,' she said bitterly. 'Lily-livered, as my father would say. You are terrified of emotional responsibility and so you've chosen to live in a deep freeze.'

He had reached her in two strides and for a moment—a terrifying moment—Cory thought he was going to hit her, but instead he pulled her into him with enough force to make her head snap back.

'So you think I'm an ice-man, Cory?' he rasped, so angry he had a job to get the words out. 'You think there is liquid ice in my veins instead of warm blood, is that it? You really don't know the first thing about men, do you? Although having seen Vivian I shouldn't be surprised about that.'

When his mouth took hers it was hard and savage and she knew—if she was anything like the heroine of a novel or a film—that she should now begin fighting like crazy. But—this was Max, and she loved him. She loved him beyond life. She didn't want to, she had never wanted to, but the more she'd found out about him— even the irritating, bad things—the deeper her love had become. Illogical, stupid, brainless— all those things could be thrown at her—but that was how it was.

She didn't know when his lips and hands stopped being punishing and became merely passionate, but it was far, far too late by then anyway. She was kissing him back, kiss for kiss, embrace for embrace, with an uninhibitedness that would have shocked her if she'd been capable of thinking about anything other than the sensations that were flooding her body with the fierceness of a stormy winter's sea crashing onto pummelled sands.

His kisses were drugging and sweet, his hands powerfully gentle and wonderfully understanding of what pleased her, and Cory was unaware the makeshift sarong had slipped to her waist until she felt the heat of his fingers on the velvet-smooth skin of her back. It was a sensual onslaught made all the more insidious by her innocence and she was too dazed and intoxicated by the wonder of these new sensations to think.

His tongue rippled along her teeth—she shivered. His hands worked magic on her silky skin—she arched in ecstasy. He let his mouth wander to her cheek, her ears, her throat, hot, burning kisses that evoked wild pleasure wherever they touched, and he took his time, nuzzling into the sweetly scented shadows of her collarbone as he murmured her name in a thick, husky voice that was an aphrodisiac in itself and druggingly erotic.

'Max. Oh, Max.' Her hands were clinging to his broad shoulders, her breath sobbing against his face. She was utterly his and they both knew it, and now he stiffened, his body language changing.

'Cory, listen to me. Listen to me a minute.'

'No.' As he raised his head she gave a little wail of protest at the different tone in his voice. 'Don't talk, not now,' she murmured frantically, and then, still in the grip of the tumultuous sensuality he had evoked, the wonder of being in the arms of the man she loved, the words that had been in her heart for so long just slipped out of their own accord. 'I love you, I do…'

She felt his reaction in every last fibre of her body although he didn't move or speak or even seem to breathe for some seconds. And then he slowly loosened her hands from his shoulders and took a step backwards, his face dark and closed and his body rigid.

'That's rubbish and you know it,' he said stonily; his eyes were hard on her face and there was something in them she couldn't fathom. 'You don't even like me half of the time.'

Cory fumbled with the cover, drawing it up over her breasts and tucking it tightly into the hollows of her armpits, her face scarlet, but she didn't take her gaze from his. She had a choice here, she thought wildly, even as she silently berated herself for her utter madness in the last few minutes. It had been bad enough to let him make love to her like that—after all she'd said, all her protestations of how she despised his lifestyle and morals—but to blurt out her feelings had been much, much worse.

She could say it had merely been a figure of speech in the circumstances in which she'd found herself—he'd understand that for some people it was almost a necessary formality preceding the act itself—or, humiliating and debasing as it would be, she could tell him the truth. The thought was crucifying.

One action would keep her in his life, if she chose to remain, and the other would definitely take her out of his orbit for good. The last thing Max Hunter wanted was a lovelorn secretary mooning over him across the filing cabinet or anywhere else for that matter.

Cory Masters, attractive and efficient secretary who was fun to chat up when he had nothing better to do, was one thing. Cory Masters in love was quite another. He'd run a mile. And then this thing, this wild, ecstatic, painful thing, would be finished. She knew which choice she was going to make before she spoke—it was the only one that would allow her to remain sane.

'No, Max, it's not rubbish,' she said with an icy calm that came from the utter numbness that had taken her over body and soul at the enormity of what she was about to do. 'I do love you; I've loved you for ages, although everything I've said about the way you conduct your life still stands.'

'But Vivian?' He glared at her, his voice as terse as if she had just slapped his face rather than told him she loved him. 'How can you say you care about me when you and him—?'

'There is no me and him,' Cory said dully. His reaction was worse than anything her darkest nightmare had conjured up. He despised her now—it was written all over his face—

whereas before she had at least had his respect. But she couldn't have done anything else, she told herself bitterly in the next instant. Things had gone too far, much too far. 'There never has been, I realise that now. What I felt for him was affection, maybe love of a brotherly kind, but that's all. If I had married him, if he'd asked me, it would have been a terrible mistake.'

'He wants you, you know that. And perhaps you would be happy with him?' he said with a terrible lack of emotion, his face cold.

He was encouraging her to go to *Vivian*? It was the final humiliation and Cory knew nothing would ever hurt as much in her life again. He was so desperate to get rid of her now she had told him how she felt that he was throwing her at Vivian. Oh, she hated him. She did, she really hated him.

'I've told you how I feel.' She raised her head proudly now, her face white except for two spots of burning colour glowing dark across her cheekbones. 'And don't worry, Max, I know you are incapable of feeling the same and I don't want anything from you. I just thought it might help you to understand why I need to resign and leave immediately, that's all. I can't play at being the sophisticated, worldly type you go for; I just don't have it in me, and frankly I don't want to be like that,' she added bravely.

'This is crazy.' Max drew in a deep breath, his face set and frighteningly cold. 'I don't believe this is happening.' He raked back a lock of hair from his forehead, the gesture betraying his iron control was only skin-deep, before he added, 'Damn it, Cory, you never said, you never indicated…'

'I never would have.' She was determined she wasn't going to cry—whatever else she was *not* going to cry and add that to her list of failings in his eyes. 'And there would have been no need for any of this if you hadn't brought me here today.'

At least he couldn't blame her for orchestrating the whole miserable event, Cory thought painfully. From beginning to end it had been Max determined to get his own way as usual. Well, this time he had got a little more than he'd bargained for, she thought, with a black humour that put a touch of very necessary strength in her trembling limbs. A darn sight more, actually.

'So…' She raised her small chin, her eyes glowing like a fierce little cat's as she willed herself not to break down until he had left. 'If I get dressed now will you order me a taxi, please?'

She was still speaking when she heard the sound of a car drawing up outside and then loud, shrill voices, followed by the ringing of the doorbell. Oh, no, not visitors, not now, she thought desperately.

'Cory.' She had never seen Max stumbling for words but she was seeing it now. 'This is what I came to tell you—' He paused, and then, as the doorbell sounded again, said, 'I've invited a few friends round for the evening. I thought after all you said this afternoon that you would prefer that, and I did promise no strings attached and no ulterior motive. I thought a party might be just what we both needed to blow away the cobwebs.'

'I see.' There was a sick flood of despair flowing through her, but she kept her voice even as she said, 'A party sounds fine to me, Max. I'll get ready and then I'll see you downstairs, shall I?' She was *not* going to crumple; she was going to handle this.

Max looked at her and she stared back at him, hoping desperately that she was masking the agony that was making her feel as if she was shrinking into a tiny nothingness, and then he nodded abruptly as the doorbell chimed for the third time and yet another car pulled up outside, and with one swift movement he turned and then was gone.

She sank straight down on to the carpet the moment the door shut, her legs refusing to hold her up a second longer, and stared blindly ahead as she tried to formulate her thoughts in the chaotic whirl her brain had become.

She *knew* she had sensed something down by the pool, she told herself silently. There had been a definite withdrawal, a detachment from that point, even though he had been quite pleasant and amusing and fun to be with for the rest of the afternoon. He had decided to wash his hands of her then, she saw it now, and he had merely come to her room this evening to tell her that the cosy, romantic dinner for two she had been expecting was not going to happen. He had invited goodness knew how many friends to join them, and nothing could have stated his intentions to revert to their old boss/secretary status more clearly.

Oh… She swayed back and forth in an agony of pain and embarrassment. And then she'd allowed… She couldn't let her mind dwell on what she had allowed. And she had further compounded the whole disastrous scenario by telling him she *loved* him.

She had wanted to cry when he had been with her, but now her eyes were quite dry, the consuming despair that was churning her stomach and making her shake too intense for the relief of tears.

When it came to making a fool of herself she had excelled beyond most mortals' wildest dreams, she told herself bitterly. And how was she going to get through this evening? For a moment—just a moment—she contemplated sneaking out of the house and making a run for it. The gates were obviously now open—yet another car had driven up while she had sat in mute misery on the carpet—so she would have no trouble in escaping.

But then the fiery strength she had inherited from her mother's red-haired genes, along with the fighting spirit her father had instilled in her from when she was a small toddler and gone through a stage of being bullied at nursery by two slightly older little girls, sprang into play. She was *not* going to skulk away like a whipped puppy, she told herself tensely. Whatever, she would see this evening out with that sophistication and control he so admired in his harem, and then, come morning, she would walk out of this house and out of his life for good. She could do it; she could.

She sat for a few more moments as she did some exercises to regulate her breathing and bring her racing heart under control, and then she rose shakily, making her way across the room and back into the bedroom. She stared for a moment at the crumpled dress on the floor.

Oh, no, no, that wouldn't do now. That dress had been chosen with a view to keeping the wolf at bay, but everything had changed now. When she walked out of his life she was going to do it with a bang not a whimper!

She scanned the wardrobe again but she already knew the little number she was going to wear. She had seen it earlier and she'd stroked the scarlet silk with an awed hand, wondering at the nerve of the woman who would dare to wear such a wildly sexy and undeniably wickedly provocative dress. She had noticed there was a pair of shoes in the same material as the dress—high, strappy sandals designed with a view to making the legs endless—and now she slipped them on anxiously. They fitted perfectly. An omen that this was meant to be. Cory nodded grimly at the thought. With a bit of luck this outfit was going to make Max's eyes stand out like chapel hatpegs!

The saying was one of her father's and for a moment it brought his comforting presence into the room, but then, as she felt the tears begin to burn the back of her eyes, she willed them away. No weakness, not now, not yet. She could cry buckets later but for now she was going to hold up her head and prove to Max Hunter she was just as sexy and desirable as any of those bimbos he ran around with! She shut her eyes tightly and took several long, deep breaths.

She had been virtually ready when Max had surprised her, but now she redid her hair, taking time to curl it into a mass of glowing waves that fell on to her shoulders in a gleaming curtain.

The cosmetics in the top drawer of the dressing table were amazing—all colours, all shades of absolutely everything—and Cory made up very carefully, accentuating the violet tinge in her green eyes with a deep blue shadow and plenty of mascara, and using a creamy red lipstick on her generous mouth.

When she slipped the dress and shoes on and then stood in front of the mirror she couldn't quite believe the reflection she saw was hers. The beautiful dress, with its flattering, low-cut neckline and fitted bodice, full skirt that ended just above her knees and swirls and swirls of red silk, had transformed her figure into something any red-blooded male would take a second look at. And Max was red-blooded; she had to give him that if nothing else. But it was the way it clung where it was meant to cling and pulled in and pushed out other parts of her anatomy that made it dynamite.

She would never say that designer clothes were a waste of money again, Cory promised silently as she sent up a prayer of thanks for the

skill that had created such a confidence-builder.
She might just get through this evening after all.
No one looking at her tonight would believe she
was harbouring a broken heart under this plunging neckline.

When Cory walked into the drawing room some
minutes later Max was at her elbow in an instant, and she turned just in time to see the flash
of desire that narrowed the amber eyes into slits
of gold light before his expression changed and
became bland.

'You look wonderful,' he said softly, but she
heard the thickness he couldn't quite mask, and
it gave her the shot in the arm she needed to be
able to say coolly in response, 'Thank you, Max.
You look pretty good yourself.' She forced herself to glance around.

Pretty good? He looked good enough to die
for, Cory thought desperately. He must have
been about to change when he'd come in to her
earlier, because the shirt and trousers he had
been wearing then had been changed for a dinner suit. The cream silk shirt was open at the
neck, however, and showing a smidgen of dark
body hair at the top of his chest, his bow tie
hanging in thin strands at either side of his
throat. He looked so sexy it made her knees
weak.

She saw him raise one hand and in the next instant a waiter was there at her elbow with a tray on which reposed several sparkling glasses of champagne.

She took one with a smile of thanks to the waiter before again glancing at the assembled crowd, more than a little surprised to see there were already about thirty people present, with more arriving judging by the sounds in the hall. This was going to be a party and a half.

'You arranged all this on the spur of the moment?' she asked quietly. 'The waiters, the catering and everything?'

'I have a firm I use for such occasions; my housekeeper prefers it that way,' Max said coolly. 'They know me and they can jump at a moment's notice; they know I'll make it worth their while. As for my friends...' he waved a casual hand but there was a cynical twist to his mouth now '...they are avid party-goers, all of them, and they like to be in the right place at the right time.'

'And you are the right place at the right time,' Cory stated flatly. Of course he was; she should have known. How the other half lived... She thought of the wealth that engendered such power. She could see more uniformed waiters moving among the throng now, and in the garden, beyond the open French doors, there was a small band setting up. No doubt there was an army of caterers seeing to the food too. Clockwork. He paid for his life to move on instantly oiled wheels and that was what he got. He didn't need her—he didn't need anyone. He just clicked his fingers and the world came to obedient heel.

'*Sweety-pie*...' The tall, voluptuous blonde was hanging on the arm of another man but it didn't stop the sultry painted eyes from devouring Max. 'It's been absolutely *ages*, darling.'

'Three weeks to be exact, Adrianne,' Max said dryly. 'You and Frank were at Charles's fortieth if I remember right?' He shook the other man's hand as he spoke and then expertly manoeuvred Cory into the side of him with a dexterity that was formidable, before adding, 'This is Cory Masters, incidentally. Cory, meet Frank and Adrianne Peers. Frank and I go way back to university days.'

Adrianne managed something that could just about be called a smile, but her eyes dissected Cory with cat-like sharpness. 'Cory...' She held out an expertly tanned, red-taloned hand. 'How sweet.'

Cory wasn't sure if she was referring to her name or the fact that it looked as though she was Max's latest girlfriend, but she smiled back—coolly and calmly—as she said, 'It's always nice to meet the wife of one of Max's old friends.' And then to Frank, who looked a nice old thing although at least twenty years older than Max, 'It's nice to meet you.'

'Masters...?' Adrianne drawled the name slowly, running it over her small white teeth like a tasty titbit. 'We know a few Masters, don't we, Frankie? Are you one of Sir Gerald's daughters, perhaps?' she asked Cory as she turned to her again.

'No, I'm not.' This was some form of attack; Cory felt it in her bones and she kept her voice steady as she added, 'My father's Christian name is Robert.'

'Really?' For whatever reason, Adrianne made it sound as though Cory's grandparents had made a grave mistake in so naming their son. 'And you're from?' She paused, her painted eyebrows enquiring.

'Yorkshire,' Cory said politely, just as Max at the side of her shifted abruptly and said, his voice cold and almost cruel. 'And my parents lived in Essex, Frank's in Bournemouth and Adrianne's in the East End of London, so I believe?' His gaze had swept over the other woman and something in it made the ravishing blonde flush scarlet. 'So, we all know everything there is to know about each other, don't we?' he added pleasantly. 'Now, Cory, there are a couple of other people I'd like you to meet, so if you'll excuse us...'

He had moved her on before Cory could even say goodbye, but she had noticed the look in the other woman's eyes and she couldn't resist asking Max what the little scene had been all about.

'Adrianne's a snob of the first order,' Max said shortly, still frowning. 'She likes to put it about that her parents have their own business on the outskirts; in reality her father is a fishmonger in the East End where they've lived all their life and Adrianne is one of ten children who were brought up hand-to-mouth. Frank said the family is great, salt of the earth, but Adrianne won't even acknowledge their existence since she married Frank and moved into the fast lane. Her real name is Annie, by the way, but she considered it too ordinary for her new status. Adrianne puts a lot of store by names,' he added wryly. 'As you may have gathered.'

'You don't like her.' It was a statement not a question.

'She's the biggest mistake Frank ever made but he doesn't see it that way.' Max shrugged irritably. 'She's played around, she spends money like water, she's greedy and avaricious, with the morals of an alley-cat. Does that answer your question?' He turned to look down at her now, smiling derisively, but she didn't answer him.

How was she going to get through this evening if he remained at her side? she asked herself with bitter despair. He was torturing her; surely he must realise that?

The torture continued for a good few hours more, and it included forcing a plateful of food—which was no doubt delicious but tasted like sawdust to Cory—down her throat, chatting with all and sundry with Max's arm glued round her waist, dancing to the small band in the summer-scented shadows of the garden and much more. Neither she nor Max said a word about what had happened earlier—he was his normal cool, urbane self and she was determined that she could match him moment for moment or die in the attempt. It was horrendous, it was awful, but somehow—somehow—she got through.

And then it was gone three in the morning and gradually the guests were taking their leave, the beautiful women in their Guccis and Versaces and Armanis just as fresh and glowing as when they had arrived, and the men all seeming to have come from one wealthy, powerful, affluent cloning process.

Cory was so mentally, emotionally and physically exhausted she felt she could sleep standing up. As the numbers dwindled to the last ten or twelve and the band began to pack up, Max ordered for coffee and croissants to be served in the dining room.

'I'm going up to my room if that's okay?' Cory met Max in the vast hall where he had been giving last instructions to the caterers. 'It's been a long day.'

'Fine.' He nodded slowly, and then she tensed as he leant forward and lightly brushed her lips with his own as he said, 'We'll have to talk, you know that, don't you? But it's not important now.'

She wasn't important. She nodded in return and then, as one of the waiters came hurrying up and spoke in fluent French—a language that held no secrets for Max—she watched him listen for a moment before he turned back to her. 'There's a problem. You don't mind...?'

'No, you go.' Go, go, *go*!

And he went.

Cory had just taken half a dozen steps up the beautiful winding staircase, wondering how she could ever find the strength to reach the top and the sanctuary of her suite, when she heard her name spoken softly behind her. It wasn't Max's voice.

She turned to see Frank at the bottom of the stairs, his eyes tight on her. She had had a couple of conversations with Max's old friend dur-

ing the evening and she liked him, very much.
He was funny and sincere and witty but, more
than that, he seemed kind, and kindness wasn't
a trait she'd noticed much in most of the assembled company. They all seemed intent on out-
doing each other in every respect.

He had gone to great lengths to explain that
his wife was really insecure and unsure of herself; a 'lost child' was the way he had described
Adrianne, whom no one understood. Cory
couldn't help but be sceptical about this;
Adrianne seemed about as unsure of herself as
a shark in a feeding frenzy, but she had accepted
his explanation for what they both knew was
Adrianne's rudeness to her with a nodding head
and a comforting pat on his arm, and the two of
them had gone on to discuss everything from
music to mythology, which was Frank's hobby.
They had discussed everything, in fact, except
Max.

'Cory?' He joined her on the stairs and she
saw he was somewhat embarrassed about something. 'Can I ask you to bear with me a moment
if I'm a little presumptuous?' he asked awk-
wardly.

'Presumptuous?' She stared into the velvet-
brown eyes set in a square face which reminded
her of her father's.

'I just felt...' He took a deep breath and then said quickly, 'It's about Max. Dare I ask you if you are in love with him?'

It was on the tip of her tongue to evade the question whilst gently indicating for him to mind his own business, but she knew it must have taken him some time to work up the courage to approach her, and so she said, after a long pause, while her tired brain tried to judge how best to answer such a loaded question, 'You must have a reason for asking that, Frank?'

'I'm Max's friend and I think a hell of a lot of him,' Frank said quietly, 'but you are one of the nicest people I've met for a long time and I wouldn't like to see you get hurt, Cory. Not without a warning anyway. You would never survive with Max, not and emerge the same person anyway. It isn't his fault but he's never satisfied for long; he gets bored and then... But he normally chooses women who know the score, and somehow... Somehow I don't think you do.'

'It's all right, Frank.' His face had gone turkey-red and she was finding she felt really sorry for him despite her own embarrassment. 'It's not like that, really.'

'He's tough, Cory.' Frank had obviously braced himself to say it all. 'He might have inherited a nice amount at the beginning, but

Hunter Operations has been built up to what it is now by his hard work and dedication. He's ruthless when he has to be and he doesn't take any prisoners. It's just the way he is.'

'Frank, I told you earlier, I'm just his secretary,' Cory said quietly, and then, when he still didn't look convinced, she added softly, 'And between the two of us I resigned today, so really I'm not even that any more.'

'You've resigned?' There was definite relief in Frank's voice, and Cory found she really couldn't be annoyed at his interference.

'He needs another Gillian,' she said painfully.

'I know what he needs.' Frank looked at her for a long moment and his eyes were understanding. 'But he's too much of a damn fool to see it or too stubborn to admit it.'

She smiled, because it was either that or bursting into tears. Frank's unexpected concern had touched her more than he would ever know. And then she reached up and kissed him gently on the cheek as she said, 'Thanks, Frank. I don't suppose I'll see you again but Max is lucky to have a friend like you.'

He continued to stand at the bottom of the stairs as she climbed the treads to the big, balcony-style landing, and she turned at the top, raising her hand to him just once before she turned and made her way to the quiet scented tranquillity of her suite.

Although she didn't feel quiet or tranquil inside, she admitted bitterly as she closed the door of the sitting room behind her and stood for a moment against the varnished wood, her eyes tightly shut and her heart thudding. She doubted if she would ever feel those things again. She felt angry and hurt and desolate.

She walked into the beautiful bedroom and switched on the mellow wall lights before walking across to the mirror. 'Well, you got through, girl,' she told the vibrant, slender woman in the mirror. 'And you did it with style, I'll say that for you.'

And then she sank down on to the carpet by the side of the bed and cried as though her heart would break.

CHAPTER NINE

NERVES almost got the better of Cory the next morning when, after just a couple of hours of restless sleep, she prepared to go downstairs for breakfast.

She was dressed in the same clothes she had arrived in, but she had borrowed some underwear from the stacked shelves in the huge walk-in wardrobe, and she was sure the brief white lacy pants and bra—with their exclusive label—would have cost ten times more than the rest of her outfit put together. It somehow seemed to sum up the whole miserable state of affairs she found herself in, she thought ruefully as she checked herself one more time in the full-length mirror, her stomach turning crazy cartwheels and her legs feeling as though they didn't belong to her.

The reflection that stared back at her bore no resemblance to the exotic flame creature of the night before, but the will to walk out of Max's life with at least the remnants of her dignity wrapped around her was as strong, and it was this feeling that enabled her to pull herself together and walk out of the room and down the stairs a few minutes later with her head held high and her back straight. Battered she might be, broken she was not.

'Good morning.' The deep dark voice was relaxed and cool.

Max was already seated at the breakfast table and he was fully dressed for the office minus his suit jacket, his black hair slicked back from his forehead and his face freshly shaven. He looked wonderful. And lazy and untroubled.

'Good morning.' Cory managed to sound brisk and cool as she returned the greeting, her eyes moving to the laden table with very real surprise. There was enough food to feed an army.

As usual Max read her mind. 'Not my work,' he said quietly. 'Mrs Brown was back from her sister's at seven this morning; her sister only lives a few miles away.'

Cory nodded, contenting herself with one dry look at the handsome face before she sat down. He had obviously thought the seduction would have been complete by morning, she thought wryly, and hadn't intended to miss his normal routine which clearly included a massive cooked breakfast just because he had thrown his poor housekeeper out of her bed the night before. Typical man, or typical Max, more like. How she could love such a cold-blooded, manipulating so-and-so she just didn't know. But she did.

Mrs Brown—a small, stout personage with cheeks like rosy red apples—came bustling in in the next moment, and the following few minutes were taken up with introductions followed by the older woman filling Cory's plate with enough food for five secretaries. Although Mrs Brown didn't think she was merely Max's secretary, did she? Cory told herself silently once they were alone again. And after a woman had shared Max's bed for the night she probably came downstairs absolutely ravenous!

The thought took away any faint appetite Cory might have had, but she struggled manfully through several rashes of bacon and two large grilled tomatoes, although the egg, sausages, mushrooms and kidneys were quite beyond her.

After his initial greeting Max had disappeared behind his paper again—which suited Cory just fine—only emerging once or twice to refill their coffee cups and ask Cory if she wanted fresh toast or anything more from Mrs Brown.

It was just as Cory thankfully pushed her plate away, feeling she had eaten enough to convince anyone—even Max—that she was fine, that the paper was lowered and put aside altogether and she found herself staring straight into

the level amber gaze. 'I want to talk to you.' It
was cool and steady and so utterly Max at his
most controlled and relaxed that she felt her
hackles rise immediately. She hadn't even made
the slightest dent in that rock-hard mind—all her
anguish, all the torment of the last twenty-four
hours was water off a duck's back as far as he
was concerned. The rat.

'Yes?' Her eyebrows rose in what she hoped
was an uninterested and bored gesture, and she
wished she had left her hair loose so she could
have tossed her head with a little more style.

'I don't want you to resign, Cory,' he said
with quiet emphasis.

No, I bet you don't, she thought viciously.
She had seen how money talked last night—an
elegant and flamboyant party thrown together at
a minute's notice in the same way most people
would hold an impromptu barbecue—and Max
had grown used to having his life flow on oiled
wheels. His secretary leaving suddenly, without
a trained replacement, would throw the side of
life he valued the most—his work—into something of a hiccup.

'I take full blame for everything that has occurred,' he continued evenly. 'I should never
have brought you here; it was totally unprofes-
sional and a bad mistake.'

Double, triple rat!

'But there is no reason why everything can't go on as it has done. You are excellent at your job, and the things you said last night... You don't mean them, Cory, not really. You don't even know me, for crying out loud. All this with Vivian, the move to the big city and a new job— a new lifestyle—it's given you a false reading of your thoughts and emotions, that's all. In a few weeks, a few months, you'll find yourself laughing at all this.'

Right, that was enough. It was bad enough she had humiliated herself so thoroughly the day before, but to have to sit and listen to him suggest she had the emotions of an adolescent schoolgirl who had a crush on her teacher was too much.

Cory straightened in her chair, her back ramrod-stiff, and she allowed nothing of what she was feeling to show in her face as she said, very clearly and very coolly, 'The matter is not open for discussion, Max. I want you to accept my resignation as of today. I will, of course, stay until you have a replacement. It was foolish of me to say anything other than that yesterday, and I know how you hate temps. I'll stay and show my replacement the ropes.'

He swore, very succinctly but with great emphasis, before grating, 'This is not about me disliking temps, woman. I don't want you to

leave!' He glared at her as though she were being obtuse.

Cory's heart turned over. The way he'd said
that, the look on his face now—it was similar
to that moment down by the pool when he had
said she was one of her own; could it be that he
had fallen for her, that he was beginning to think
of her as something more than just a quick tum-
ble in bed?

'Why?' she asked softly. 'Why don't you
want me to leave?'

He stared at her for a moment, and she had
never called on so much will-power as in this
moment when she continued to look back at him
without allowing the raging turmoil and soaring
hope to show, and then the mask he could adopt
at will slid into place and his eyes narrowed, his
mouth thinning, as he said, 'I've told you, you
are excellent at your job. And we get on well;
I like having you around.' And he thought that
would persuade her to stay?

'And I'm not boring?' It was flat and dull.

'That too,' he agreed expressionlessly.

Damn you, Max Hunter.

She rose from the chair, her expression as un-
readable as his. 'Sorry, it's not enough,' she said
quietly. 'Come four weeks from now I'm walking, Max, so you'd better get looking for my
replacement because I'm not being strung along.

I'll work with her to make the change-over as easy as possible—as many hours a day as you like—but that's as far as I'm going. Okay?'

'You won't just drop into another job,' he rasped impatiently. 'Surely you see that?'

'That's my problem, not yours,' she said stiffly.

'You intend to run home to lover-boy, is that it?'

'What I do or don't do is absolutely nothing to do with you, Max.' How dared he, how *dared* he suggest that?

He had been in the motion of standing but now he stilled, his eyes searched her closed face for one long moment before he straightened. Cory found she was holding her breath, her heart thudding, as they continued to stare at each other for what seemed an endless amount of time, and then Max nodded, his voice deliberately cold as he said, 'You're absolutely right of course. Very well, Cory, I accept your resignation. Perhaps you'd get on to the agencies we use once we're back in the office and get things moving. Weed out the best three they've got on their books and I'll do the final interviews.' He held her eyes one moment more and then turned.

'Fine.' Cory was pale and shaking as he marched from the room. He hadn't fallen for her—how could she have been so ridiculous as to imagine it even for a minute? she asked herself numbly. He would never fall for her. Oh, fancy her maybe, perhaps even enjoy her company—he'd said he liked having her around after all. But then people liked having dogs and cats and budgerigars around, she reminded herself harshly, but it didn't make them want to marry them. Not that she'd thought of marriage and Max being compatible anyway.

She continued standing there for a few moments more until the entrance of Mrs Brown moved her towards the open door leading to the hall. Once in her suite of rooms she collected her handbag and jacket and then went quickly downstairs to wait by the front door without glancing in the mirror.

He wanted her—or he wanted her body, to be more precise—but strictly on his own terms. End of story. End of job. And just at the moment it felt like the end of the world.

The next four weeks were harder than anything Cory had faced in her life before but she learnt quite a bit about herself.

The agencies fell over themselves to be helpful, but due to the fact that her replacement was needed immediately, and most of the women on their books were either in employment with a

designated notice period to work out or not up
to the calibre Max would demand of his secretary, the choice was limited.

However, within a few days of giving her resignation Cory had lined up three interviews—
one with a twenty-six-year-old stunner who
looked like a supermodel and had qualifications
coming out of her beautiful ears, the second
with an ice-cool blonde who looked as though
she could handle Max Hunter as easily as blinking, and the third with a buxom, motherly type
who was going on fifty and had just been made
redundant after working twenty years for the
same managing director when the firm had gone
into liquidation.

The wild relief and joy Cory felt when Max
chose the last applicant slowly trickled away as
cold reason set in. It didn't matter whom he
chose, not really. She would never see him
again after she left Hunter Operations, she told
herself on the Friday night of her second week
of training the very able Bertha Cox, and soon
all this would be just a memory. She had to be
sensible about this.

After a wretched night's sleep she woke on
the Saturday morning feeling she could be more
sensible if she had some tender loving care, and
by nine o'clock she had thrown her overnight

bag in the back of the Mini and was on her way home to confide in her parents.

Her parents were wonderful, but she had known they would be. They sat and talked sense for hours, they kept all visitors at bay and they spoilt her rotten, but it was on the Sunday lunchtime, just as her father was carving the succulent roast, that he glanced across at Cory and said, 'I've got it! Of course. Aunt Mildred's cottage. It'd do you the world of good.'

'Aunt Mildred's cottage?' Cory stared at him and then winced as Vivian's unmistakable rat-tat-tat sounded at the front door. Since he had seen her Mini on the Saturday morning he had been round five times, and she had had to be quite rude to him the day before to get him to leave, telling him what she thought of him in the process.

'I'll get rid of him.'

As her mother scurried to the front door her father turned again to Cory, his voice lower as he repeated, 'Aunt Mildred's cottage in Shropshire,' as though that explained everything.

'What about it?' Cory asked patiently.

'She's on a cruise, for three months or so—wasting all her money, the daft old bat, but that's another story—and she said any of the family can use the cottage for a holiday while she's away. It's just what you need—a bit of peace and quiet and a chance to recharge the batteries.' Her father beamed at her.

'Dad, I don't think—'

'You said you wanted a break before you look for another job and the change will do you good. You've got enough money to cover the rent for your bedsit for a couple of months?' he asked quietly.

Cory nodded slowly. Her bank balance was very healthy.

'There you are, then; it'll be waiting for you when you go back to London after the wedding.'

Cory almost said, 'What wedding?' before she remembered and gave an inward groan. She'd need a holiday to stand that fiasco.

'Think about it, lass. You need a break, the cottage is free, and if you come back here Vivian'll give you no peace.'

Cory did think about it, but she only made her mind up about the cottage on her last day at Hunter Operations. It was the day she had been dreading, and for weeks her mind had played a hundred different scenarios as to how it would go, but the reality was ten times worse. A hundred, a million times worse.

Max had been nothing more than the original ice-man for days, which had made things terribly awkward more than once with Bertha Cox around—the other woman had taken to looking at them both very strangely—but up until five o'clock on the Friday evening Cory thought she had handled it all very well.

And then, just as she had slipped into her jacket preparatory to leaving the office with Bertha, Max put his head round the interconnecting door. 'I'd like a word before you go, Cory.' It was abrupt and cold and it sent the butterflies in her stomach—which had been having a whale of a time all day—into a fresh frenzy as he disappeared back into his office.

'I'll say goodbye now, Cory. I've got the family round for dinner tonight so I want to get away sharpish,' Bertha said quickly, giving her a brief hug and then scuttling out of the door before Cory could object, her grey hair bobbing agitatedly.

Brilliant. Thanks a bunch, Bertha. Cory's eyes were rueful as they stared at the fast closing door, but she really couldn't blame the other woman. Max at his coldest was formidable.

She took a long, deep breath, prayed that the heat staining her cheeks wasn't too obvious, and then knocked once on the interconnecting door before opening it wide. 'You wanted a word?' she asked formally.

The first thing she noticed was the bottle of champagne and two glasses. The second—the ice-man had disappeared and in his place was a warm, sexy hunk with a come-hither smile and eyes the colour of molten gold. Her heart gave a mighty kick against her ribcage and then bolted and her stomach turned right over.

'You didn't think I'd let you go like this, did you?' he asked softly, and then, as she continued to stand in the doorway, her eyes drowning pools of jade, he added, 'Come and sit down, Cory.'

'I don't want to sit down.' It wasn't true— her legs had gone to jelly but to sit down would mean she had agreed to listen to him.

'Please?' He had risen and taken the few steps to her side as he'd spoken and now he took her arm, his fingers gentle, and ushered her across to the seat in front of his desk, where he further compounded the problems with her breathing by perching nonchalantly in front of her, his trousers pulling tight across hard male thighs.

'Here.' He deftly poured her a glass of champagne, handing it to her with another devastating smile before turning slightly and pouring one for himself. 'A toast,' he said softly.

'To what?' She was hoping, desperately, that the impossible had become possible and he had discovered he couldn't live without her, even as the cold voice of reason warned her she was crazy.

'To us, of course.' His voice was low and husky and it trickled over her taut nerves like warm honey. 'You aren't my secretary any more, I'm not your boss. We're just two ordinary people who would like to get to know each other better. We can take it as slow as you like now, nothing heavy, you'll see. You can't deny the attraction between us, Cory, but in time you'll see it for what it is.'

'You mean I'll see I don't love you,' she stated quietly, her heart thumping. 'But I won't, Max, so what then? What will you say then? Sorry, Cory, but I did warn you of what to expect? Because you have, haven't you? You've laid it all on the line and given yourself the get-out clause way in advance.'

'It's not like that,' he said roughly, his eyes darkening.

'That's exactly what it's like.'

'Cory, listen to me.' He reached out for her glass and put it on the desk beside him before drawing her to her feet and into his arms. She didn't move and she didn't try to fight him, but she could have been a block of stone for all the response she gave as he moved her in close. 'I want you; I want you so badly I can't think of anything else,' he whispered huskily, 'and I know you want me too. It's crazy to deny us both.'

She wanted to remain still and distant, aloof from the frightening magnetic pull, but as the warmth of his lips found hers she shuddered helplessly. He was holding her so tightly she could scarcely breathe, her softness fitting into the hard frame of his body as though it were the last perfect piece in a jigsaw. His mouth crushed hers, the desire that had him in its thrall making him hungry for every little bit of her.

A wave of heat swept over her, burning up all the common sense and cool logic that had reiterated—time and time again over the last four miserable weeks—exactly why it would be nothing short of emotional suicide to get involved with Max. She loved him; she loved him so much. Perhaps it would be better to take anything he could give for as long as he could give it and not look to the future? Other women managed it and survived.

His kisses were becoming deeper and hungrier, his hands moving with controlled assurance as they touched and teased and brought exquisite frissons of pleasure wherever they roamed. She knew her body was betraying her need of him just as his arousal was doing the same, his manhood rock-hard against the soft swell of her belly. Her breathing had gone hay-wire; she was gasping and panting and the blood was singing through her veins like a warm flood, but there was something—some little echo of reason which had been born out of the misery of the last few weeks—that stopped her from capitulating fully to his unspoken demands.

He was offering her passion and an affair, not love and commitment, and he was determined it wouldn't be any different. The door to his heart was closed—it had been closed a long, long time now—and perhaps the key was lost for ever, but without his heart she had nothing. It wasn't that she wanted him to express declarations of undying devotion or ask her to marry him, Cory told herself silently. But she did want him to be open to whatever they might find together, that was all. But he wouldn't be. He *couldn't* be. She had to face it, let him go and get on with her life. So she had better open her mouth and tell him just that.

He sensed the change in her a few seconds later, raising his head to look down into her face from which all colour had fled. 'Cory?' he asked softly. 'What is it?'

'I can't be what you want me to be, Max, and I love you too much to try. Please, please don't contact me again because I won't change my mind.' She had to do this; she had to make it crystal-clear because if she didn't finish this now—cut off all avenues—he would keep trying to seduce her into his bed. And one day, in a moment of need and weakness, she might succumb.

'I don't believe that.' His voice was quiet but there was an edge of anger there too, and she understood why. He was so used to having his cake and eating it that he couldn't believe someone had taken away the spoon.

'You're going to have to,' she said softly as she pushed away from him. 'Because I'm not going to change my mind.'

He let her go, his hands dropping at his sides as he stared at her with a most peculiar look on his handsome face. Bewilderment was there, along with irritation and surprise, but there was something else she couldn't fathom deep in the dark amber of his eyes. He thrust his hands deep into his pockets, frowning darkly.

'Do you think this is going to make me change my mind?' he asked coldly after a long moment when he had stood and watched her adjust her clothing. 'You can't blackmail me, Cory.'

'Blackmail you?' The pain and anguish that were tearing her apart were swallowed up in a fury that had her glaring at him as her eyes shot green sparks. '*Blackmail* you!'

'Yes, blackmail me,' he said tightly. 'What else do you call this? If you're holding out for a wedding ring—'

'*That's enough.*' It was a soft snarl and to give Max his due he had the sense to stop. 'You don't see, you really don't see, do you?' Cory said after a tense moment when she called on all her strength not to leap at him and bite and scratch and pummel that handsome face she loved so much. 'Max, I wouldn't marry you if you were the last man on earth,' she bit out painfully, her voice shaking. 'I love you, I think I'll always love you, but I'm not going to let you destroy me, and marriage with you would be a nightmare. Something in you has got distorted and warped; you are locked away inside yourself and you aren't man enough to come out into the light and take a chance like the rest of us. I'm not trying to blackmail you, I'm trying to tell you goodbye.'

She turned as she spoke, walking to the door and standing in the aperture where she turned to face him for the last time. 'The way you were brought up was hard, and what happened with Laurel was awful, but it was years ago, Max. Years ago. You are going to end up a bitter, lonely, forsaken old man if you aren't careful.' Her voice was devoid now of anger but very grim.

She was waiting for a come-back, one of the ruthlessly cutting remarks he was so good at or a verbal assault that would dissect and serrate, but he was completely silent and still, only the black fury in his dark face betraying his anger.

She didn't say goodbye; there was no point after all—their goodbyes had all been said that painful morning at his house weeks ago. She simply turned and stepped out into the adjoining office, shutting the door quietly behind her and then walking with careful measured steps out of the room and into the corridor beyond.

Right until she was outside in the busy London street Cory half expected him to come after her. It couldn't end like this, she told herself as she forced her legs to keep moving, hardly aware of the crowded pavements and the thick, sluggish August air. She *loved* him; how was she going to get through the rest of her life without him? And now he hated her; she had seen it in the glittering gold eyes and the way his mouth had pulled into a thin white line in the angry tautness of his face.

But perhaps this was the only way it could have ended? The thought was unwelcome but she knew it to be the truth. Nothing else could have convinced him to leave her alone. He had seen her as something of a challenge, she was sure of that, and added to that monstrous ego and razor-sharp intelligence was a very definite leader-of-the-pack type determination to subjugate and conquer.

She was walking blindly, her eyes desperate, and when she had bumped into three people in as many seconds she realised she had to get control of herself. She stood at the side of a shop doorway, breathing deeply and forcing the air into her lungs, and slowly the mad pounding in her head and buzzing in her ears lessened.

She would go to Aunt Mildred's cottage, she told herself numbly as she slowly began to walk again. If nothing else it would give her a breathing space before the next hurdle—Vivian and Carole's wedding. And then after that... After that she would have to face the rest of her life. And right now she just couldn't imagine how she would do that.

CHAPTER TEN

IT WAS three weeks later, the middle of September, and Cory had spent all that time at Aunt Mildred's tranquil, peaceful retreat.

She had fled there the night she had left Max's office, her heart in shreds, and apart from a couple of telephone calls to her parents—Aunt Mildred didn't have a telephone: horrible, intrusive machines that embodied the worst of the twentieth century, according to her elderly aunt—and several excursions to the small village shop some three miles away she had spoken to no one. And it had been just what she needed.

She had spent warm, lazy days in the open air, tramping the lanes and open fields and valleys around her aunt's quaint little cottage, taking the paths by the river where water splashed in tiny natural fountains over time-washed rocks and where the rat-tat-tat of woodpeckers and their occasional lunatic cry could be heard.

She'd lain in green grassy meadows carpeted with daisies and cornflowers and wild orchids and campions, listening to the larks singing as

269

they swooped and soared in the blue arch of the sky before she'd eaten the apple and chocolate she'd brought with her, then walked some more in the grass-scented air.

And then, as the evening shadows had begun to fall in the hedgerows and byways, she had made her way home to The Honeypot—Aunt Mildred's cottage—eating her evening meal of home-cured ham and salad, or chicken and new potatoes and vegetables, in her aunt's wonderful country garden, where honeysuckle romped up the trees and the evening resounded with bird-song, blackbirds, thrushes, robins, finches and a little jenny-wren—the noisiest of them all—all competing to sing the loudest.

Each morning had dawned sunny and warm and Cory had risen with the sun, looking with gratitude at the deep blue sky flecked with the cotton wool of fluffy white clouds as she had blessed the absent Aunt Mildred whose open-handed benevolence had allowed her such a sanctuary in which to lick her wounds.

At first she had tossed and turned the nights away, her heart sore and her mind heavy, but gradually the magic of the place had poured in a healing balm and she had begun to take each day as it came, not thinking too much, not con-templating the future, just being.

It couldn't last, she knew that, but it had been the safety valve she'd so desperately needed, and in this idyll, set apart from the rest of the world and normal life, she had managed to relax and step out of time. The sun had brought a honey-glow to her skin, deepened the rich red tints in her dark silky hair and softened the look of agony staring out of her eyes.

She had thought of Max—all the time at first and then, as the hot lazy days had worked their spell, just most of the time—and gone through the cycle of endless post-mortems that females were so good at, but within a few days she had come to the conclusion that she couldn't have acted any differently and remained half sane. And with that knowledge the peace had come. It didn't help the pain and loss, but it gave her the strength to relax, soak up the soothing ambience of the secluded haven and allowed her to prepare for the time when she would have to leave and go back into the real world.

And now that time was here.

Cory rose from the little garden bench surrounded by climbing roses and catmint and the hum of fat honeybees where she had eaten her breakfast each morning, and looked at the cottage garden dozing in the mild September sunshine one more time. Tomorrow was Vivian and

Carole's wedding day and she couldn't delay
any longer. Her holiday was over.

'You look beautiful, Carole. Absolutely beautiful.'

Cory had just put the finishing touches to
Carole's headdress and veil, tweaking the band
of tiny fresh pink rosebuds nestled in green
leaves and lace into place and making sure the
clouds of chiffon that fell into cascading layers
to the floor were securely gripped into the pretty
blonde's fluffy hair.

'Thank you.' The other girl was already
misty-eyed and weepy with emotion. The two
of them were in Cory's bedroom at home—her
mother had offered for Carole and the bridesmaids to leave from their home due to the fact
that Carole had no family and was in lodgings—
and now Carole leant forward and gripped
Cory's hands as she said, her voice shaky, 'And
thank you for not taking Vivian back, Cory. You
could have, I know that, but once he realised
you weren't interested we got things sorted.
We'll be happy; I know we will.'

'Oh, Carole.' Cory hadn't realised Vivian's
fiancée had known about his pre-wedding
nerves, and now her voice was very firm and
genuine when she said, 'I think he's very lucky
to get you; I mean that.' And she did too. What-

ever else, Carole loved her fiancé and she showed it unashamedly. They would make the marriage work.

There was no time to say more; the other two bridesmaids—a ten-year-old cousin of Vivian's and her teenage sister—bustled in in their layers of pink chiffon and it was time to leave for the church in the first of the two wedding cars.

The morning had been hectic, with a hundred and one little panics which hadn't been helped by the previous spell of hot weather having broken into drizzling rain, but now a weak sun was making itself felt and the air was warm and scented.

Cory had taken only the most perfunctory look at herself—the fussy bell-shaped dress with its flounces of lace and rosebuds and bows didn't suit her and she knew it—but now, as the car drew up outside the winding path to the church door, she forced a bright smile on her face for the waiting photographer.

It didn't matter that she looked faintly ridiculous, she assured herself in the moment before the car door was opened. This was Carole's day and she was every inch the radiant bride. Anyway, what was the ignominy of resembling a squashed meringue—and a pink one with rosebuds and frills to boot—compared to the fact that she would never see Max again? She would wear real meringue for the rest of her life if it would make him love her, she thought fiercely as she stepped out on to the pavement, clutching the round ball of flowers Carole had insisted the bridesmaids carry instead of the conventional posies.

And then she raised her eyes and saw the big dark man standing to one side of the church wall, and she froze.

'Come on, dear; it's supposed to be the bride who gets the jitters.' The photographer was nattering away but Cory didn't even hear him, and it was only when the other two bridesmaids pushed her from behind as they too scrambled out of the car that Cory moved on legs from which all strength had fled.

'We'll have a couple at the top of the path, near the church door, all right?' The photographer was all wide smiles and teeth. 'We want to show those lovely dresses off to the full, don't we?'

As the other two simpered and giggled Cory prayed the ground would open and swallow her. She looked awful, really awful, and although it hadn't mattered a minute ago at this second it was all she could think of.

'Cory?' His voice was deep and low and it made her shiver.

She had lowered her head and aimed to brush past Max and the rest of the crowd who had gathered at the perimeter stone wall of the church grounds, but now she felt a warm hand on her arm and she was forced to look up into his waiting eyes.

'What are you doing here?' she asked shakily, her heart kicking against her ribs with enough force to dislodge at least a ton of meringue. 'You shouldn't be here.'

'Waiting to see you,' he said softly. 'And yes, I should.'

'Max, this is crazy. We've said all that could possibly be said and this isn't fair...'

'I know,' he murmured quietly, his eyes eating her—meringue and bows and all. 'It *is* crazy and it isn't fair; you deserve far better than me. I've been looking for you for the last three weeks; did your father tell you? I've been going crazy.'

'My father?' She stared at him as though he were mad. 'You've spoken to my father?' This was turning into Alice in Wonderland.

'He wouldn't tell me where you were and he warned me off in pretty strong terms,' Max said wryly. 'I don't blame him; if you were my daughter I'd have done exactly the same thing. But I looked in your personnel records and saw when you'd requested a week's holiday for this wedding, so...I tried to be patient.'

'Max, I haven't the faintest idea what you're talking about,' Cory managed shakily. She knew she was trembling, she just couldn't control the shivers that were taking her over, but she hoped he—along with everyone else—would think it was bridesmaid's nerves. This finding her meant nothing, not really. She *knew* what he felt about her and love and commitment and everything. Nothing had changed. It was just Max unable to believe that he hadn't got what he wanted for once.

'Cory, we have to talk. You see that, don't you?'

'*Please,* dear.' The photographer had galloped back down the path from the church door where the other two bridesmaids were waiting, his round, effeminate face exasperated and perspiring. 'The bride will be arriving soon and I need to take some pictures. Can't you talk to this gentleman later?'

'This gentleman wants to talk to her now.' Max had rounded on the poor little man in much the same way as a panther who had had his tail trodden on, but the photographer wasn't having any of it. This was his art and he wasn't having anyone—even this big six-footer—messing it up. He glared at Max bravely.

'You're going to spoil the photographs,' he trilled tightly.

'Damn the photographs!' For the first time Max sounded like Max.

'Max, please leave me alone.' Cory cut into the exchange—which had drawn more interest and flapping ears from the crowd than ever a straightforward wedding could—her voice sharp now. 'This is Carole's day and you're going to ruin it, and I don't want to see you again.' Oh, my darling, my darling, my darling...

'Yes, you do.' No one was even breathing in their vicinity now. 'You love me.' It was soft and tender and very firm.

She stared into the painfully handsome, dear, dear face for one long moment, knowing she would never love anyone else the way she loved him, and then she said, her own voice firm now but with a catch in it that caused more than one female listener to sympathise, 'Stay away from me, Max. I mean it.' Then she allowed the photographer, who was positively dancing with agitation, to lead her away.

The wedding service was the sort of unmitigated nightmare Cory wouldn't have wished on her worst enemy but somehow she got through it, and no one—seeing her smiling face and calm composure—would have guessed she was falling apart inside. But that was what it felt like.

Why, oh, why had he come here like this to-day? Cory asked herself a hundred times through the next half an hour. She didn't dare turn round once and see if Max had followed her into the church. She wouldn't put it past him—she wouldn't put *anything* past him, she told herself silently. She tried—she really, *really* tried—to work up some healthy rage at his au-dacity, but the shock of seeing him again, the wonder, the fierce stupid joy she had felt in the split second she had met those beautiful amber eyes, got in the way.

And it frightened her. It frightened her more than she would have thought possible. *Nothing had changed.* If she told herself it once she told herself it a million times during the hymns and prayers and long—somewhat drawn-out—ad-dress by Vivian's uncle. A relationship with Max would be extremes of highs and lows, wild, ecstatic happiness or deep, dark black despair, and when it ended—when *he* ended it, she wouldn't know who she was or how to go on. He would eat her up and spit her out and then simply go on with his life as before. Impossible. Completely impossible. She would never sur-vive him leaving.

But he *had* cared enough to come looking for her. She caught and held the thought, shutting her eyes as her stomach turned over and she gripped the ball of flowers so hard a few freesia heads dropped to the floor.

But that was just because he wanted her in his bed, she reminded herself desperately the next moment, when she opened her eyes as the last strains of 'Love divine, all loves excelling' drifted away. When it came to satisfying their physical desire most men's brains were situated a good deal lower than their heads, and nothing in Max's history had indicated he was any different. Just the opposite in fact.

Oh, it wasn't *fair* he had come today like this. Over the last three weeks—if she had allowed herself the brief indulgence of imagining them meeting up again—she had always pictured herself beautifully dressed and groomed, the very essence of cool femininity and elegance, and here she was dressed like the fairy on top of the Christmas tree with her hair frizzed and riddled with pink—*pink*—rosebuds and her face painted like a china doll. She felt utterly, utterly ridiculous.

Perhaps it would put him off? She found the thought wasn't as comforting as it should be. Perhaps he'd gone already? The pain sliced through her with enough sharpness to make her gasp. And still the service went on. And on. And on.

By the time a triumphant Carole swept down the aisle with her Vivian to the chords of the rousing 'Bridal March', Cory was working on automatic. She followed on John's—the best man's—arm, smiling, nodding and not looking to left or right, and once outside in the gentle September sunshine she went through the endless photographs without allowing her eyes to search the watching crowd. She simply didn't dare.

The reception was being held in the village hall, which was only a stone's throw from the church and didn't require the use of the wedding cars, and it was only as the last photographs were taken and most of the guests had already wended their way there to wait for the entrance of the bride and groom that Cory saw the pure lines of a deep red Ferrari parked on the far side of the church green. A Ferrari. Here. Today.

It had to be him. She didn't know where the Rolls was, but that just had to be Max. It was.

As Cory and the other two bridesmaids approached the car the door swung open and a long, lean body uncoiled itself from the leather interior. 'Cory?' he said softly. 'Wait a moment.'

The hall was just across the cobbled road, and Cory pointed, clutching the ridiculous ball with one hand, as she said, 'I've…I've got to go in there. They're waiting.'

'I'm not going to go away.' It was cool and controlled and very calm. 'Not now, not ever. I mean it, Cory.'

She stared up at him, utterly unable to speak. There had been a note in his voice—a connotation to the words—that she dared not let herself believe was real but she wanted to cry.

The other two pink meringues shifted restlessly at her side and now Cory forced herself to say, her tone as steady as she could make it, 'Jennifer, Susan, this is Max—a…friend of mine. Max, this is Jennifer and Susan.'

'Hi.' He bestowed a brief smile on the two girls who were clearly smitten, and then, taking Cory's arm, he said, 'I'm borrowing her for a couple of minutes, okay?' as he whisked her aside.

'No, Max, it's not okay!'

As he pulled her away from the other two and frog-marched her firmly over the green to a small wooden bench set under a rich dark beech tree Cory was protesting strongly, and he looked down at her for one moment as he growled, 'Tough.'

'Who do you think you are anyway?' She was trying to be strong, she really was, but he looked so darn gorgeous, Cory thought bemusedly even as she spoke the words. The charcoal trousers and black leather jacket he was wearing accentuated his height and dark, magnetic appeal tenfold, but it wasn't that which kept her on the bench when he sat down at the side of her and began to speak. It was his voice—the slightly uneven note that betrayed the nerves he was trying to hide—and the fact that the look in his eyes was a reflection of the agony she had seen in the mirror so often over the last three weeks.

'Listen to me, Cory, please listen.' It was quiet and shaky and the rest of the world disappeared. 'I love you; I should have said that the first second I saw you again,' he said raggedly. 'But I've never said it before and it doesn't come easy.'

'No.' She shook her head as she spoke, dislodging one of the rosebuds which fell into her lap. 'No, you don't; you know you don't. Please don't say that.' *She wasn't going to cry.*

'I do love you, Cory.' His voice was fierce now, painfully fierce. 'Damn it, you have to believe me even if it takes me the rest of my life to convince you. I've known for weeks and I've been fighting it just as long, but I can't fight it any more. I want you, Cory. Not just for a week or a month or a year; I want you for the rest of my life. Forever.'

'No.' The anguish of all she had suffered was in her face as she whispered, 'You tried to make me go back to Vivian when I told you how I felt; that's not love.' It wasn't until this moment that she realised just how much he had hurt her when he had done that, and the pain was still as fierce as ever.

'I would never have let you.' It was a deep groan. 'I was still trying to convince myself you were just like all the rest. I was running scared, Cory, but I'd have killed him before I would have let him touch you. What I feel for you...' He drew in a hard, shuddering breath, shaking his head. 'It consumes me, it eats me up. I've never in all my life imagined feeling like this and I don't like it.'

The last was said with such bewilderment that for a moment she almost weakened. But she didn't believe him; she didn't dare believe him. She had seen him in operation—she had watched that ruthless mind bulldoze and manipulate and steer lesser mortals to his will too many times.

'How do you know it's love you feel?' she asked tremblingly. 'You don't believe in love, you told me. What's happened to make you change your mind?'

'You've happened,' he said softly. 'You happened and then you left me and that's when I
knew I couldn't live without you. I can't, Cory,
I mean it, but, like I said, it scares me to death.
I'm not an easy man to be with, I know that,
and I don't know how to handle this. I know
what I feel, but the rest... I've never had someone of my own to love, I don't know *how* to,
for crying out loud, but I can't be without you
either. The last three weeks have been hell.' The
words were a groan from the heart of him.

She looked into his eyes, into the golden orbs
that could be so hard and challenging but were
now desperate and wistful and glowing with
something that melted her heart. Suddenly it
was all so simple. He had come for her. *He had
come for her.*

'I love you, Cory,' he said again, his voice
shaky. 'I don't know how I'm going to prove it
to you or make you understand. I want us to
grow old together, to have children and dogs
and cats and the whole caboodle, but it's like
this great giant step into the unknown. Hell, I'm
not saying this right.'

'Max—'

'No, don't say anything, not until you've let
me convince you,' he interrupted passionately.
'You said marriage to me would be a nightmare
and you might well be right, but all I can say is

that I can promise you I'll never stop loving you. That's the one thing—the only thing at the moment—I do know. And I'd be yours, Cory— heart, soul, body and mind.'

'*Max—*'

'You can send me away but I'll keep coming back.' He was both winsome and pleading and fiercely aggressive in a way only Max could be. 'I've wanted women in my time and the wanting was easy but I'm ashamed to say it meant little. This loving…' His voice was unsteady. 'This is something else. This tears you apart inside and rips the guts out of you, but still the not having it is worse than all the pain.'

'Do you think I don't know that?' Cory asked softly.

'When you left the office that day I realised what a fool I'd been,' he said huskily. 'I went round to the flat but you weren't there, and then I suffered the torments of the damned thinking you'd gone back to him, that I'd driven you into his arms again.' His voice revealed a little of just what he'd suffered.

'There is no "again."' Cory knew he'd assumed she'd slept with Vivian, maybe other boyfriends, too, and she also knew he had liked his women experienced and well-versed in the arts of lovemaking in the past. She just didn't know how he would react to what she was going to tell him so she said it quickly, before she chickened out. 'Max, I never slept with Vivian; I've never slept with anyone.'

'You haven't?' She had astounded him—she could see it in the stunned golden gaze—but she also saw something else that made her heart leap. A fierce gratitude, a deep possessive glint that told her he was more than a little pleased with this latest development. It didn't matter! It didn't matter that she couldn't match those others in expertise.

'You're mine, Cory.' A muscle was jerking at the side of his jaw and his face was taut. 'I came here to tell you that, and that I love you, and...and to ask for your forgiveness.' He had been careful not to touch her since they had sat down but now, at the sound of her name being called out through the air, he took her face in his hands, his eyes urgent. 'You can't say no, Cory. Please, you have to give me another chance.'

She wasn't aware she was crying until his thumbs gently brushed the tears from her cheeks, and then she laughed shakily, her mouth trembling as she whispered, 'The boss is always right?'

He stared at her for a moment and she saw the shadow of uncertainty deep in the amber eyes, which made her love him all the more. 'Cory?'

'I love you, Max.' She answered him in the only way possible. 'And I'll teach you how to show your love to me and to our children and to our children's children…'

And then she was in his arms and their mouths met, clinging together as their bodies strained and merged as though they were already one. The kiss was sweet and intense and—considering that they were sitting on a small wooden bench in the middle of the church green at two o'clock on a September afternoon—disgracefully intimate, but Cory didn't care. He loved her. He loved her! And he had looked for her and waited… Oh, Max.

'You'll marry me soon?' He had wrenched his mouth away just long enough to ask. 'Very soon?'

'Scared you'll chicken out if you don't get it over with quickly?' she teased huskily against the hard, firm lips that evoked such pleasure it was difficult to breathe.

'Oh, no.' The amber eyes glowed with enough love to satisfy her for the rest of her life. 'But I want the other wolves kept at bay. You are too beautiful and desirable not to have a gold band on the third finger of your left hand.'

Beautiful and desirable? Her mascara had run, her nose was probably the same shocking pink as the wretched dress and she could feel more curls and rosebuds coming adrift even as they spoke. But he thought she was beautiful and desirable. She smiled, her face glowing and her eyes shining in a way that made Max's heart thud.

He really was a boss in a million, but as a husband he was going to be pure dynamite...

And so it proved.